LITTLE SILENT STRANGER

Little Silent Stranger

Georgiana Germaine Series, #13

By *New York Times & USA Today*
Bestselling Author

CHERYL BRADSHAW

For my stepdaughter Macey
You have all my love in this life and in the next, where the two of us
will meet again one day.

"I am rather inclined to silence, and whether that be wise or not, it is at least more unusual nowadays to find a man who can hold his tongue than to find one who cannot."
Abraham Lincoln

1

Audrey Ashford sat in front of her vanity mirror, applying a bit of color to her cheeks as she hummed along to Coldplay's "Speed of Sound" playing through the speakers of her stereo. Pleased with her overall look, she set the makeup brush to the side and stood, switching the music off. She walked to the window, her breath fogging the glass as she stared out at a dull, overcast sky. Grabbing her jacket out of the closet, she shut her bedroom door and headed downstairs.

She found her mother in the kitchen, chopping vegetables for the casserole she was making for a neighbor who'd just had a baby. A warm, savory fragrance of basil and garlic lingered in the air, and Audrey almost wished she wasn't leaving.

Her mother glanced up and said, "Are you headed over to Talia's house?"

"I am. We're finalizing plans for our college send-off party."

Her mother nodded, wiping her hands on a dish towel. "Are you driving or walking?"

"I've been cooped up in my room all day, and I think it

would be good to get some fresh air, so I'll walk. Talia will drive me home when we're finished."

"Are you going along the street or cutting through the woods?"

"The woods."

"All right. Well, be careful. It gets dark fast this time of year."

"I know. I will."

"When do you expect you'll be home?"

"I don't know, ten or eleven."

"Text me when you're on your way."

Audrey smiled, nodding. "Will do."

In a month's time, Audrey would leave for college, and she couldn't help but wonder if her mother would still ask her to check in then.

When she stepped outside, the air was cool, settling around her like a soft blanket. She hurried through the side yard, heading toward the familiar path through the woods, a shortcut she'd taken hundreds of times. She loved taking this route, through the groves of trees, being one with nature.

Her shoe crunched down on smatterings of dry leaves, a steady rhythm that almost always soothed her. Tonight, though, the woods felt different and uneasy.

As she pulled her jacket tighter around herself, somewhere in the silence a twig snapped, and the hairs on the back of Audrey's neck pricked up.

"Hello?" Audrey called. "Is anyone there?"

There was no answer, just the steady rustle of the breeze.

She glanced around, seeing no one, and convinced herself the noise she heard was just a deer or a raccoon, two of the forest's frequent visitors.

Audrey had been honest with her mother when she'd said she was going to Talia's to do some party planning, but that wasn't the only reason she was visiting her friend. There was a secret she'd been carrying, heavy and suffocating, the weight of it pressing on her with every step. As she thought about seeing Talia, the person she trusted most, she still wasn't sure she was ready to share it yet.

But if not now, when?

And what would happen once she did, and the truth had been revealed?

A faint crack echoed nearby, much too deliberate to be a branch snapping under the weight of an animal, and Audrey froze, her heart pounding in her chest like a warning she could not outrun. Another rustle came from deeper in the shadows, and Audrey's eyes darted through the trees, watching and waiting.

Now she was sure she wasn't alone.

Something or someone was in her surroundings, hidden but there, nonetheless.

Audrey moved faster, hastening her steps until she was almost at a swift jog.

One more minute, and Talia's house would come into view, rising over the ridge.

Two more minutes, and she'd be safe.

Or so she believed until a figure stepped out from behind a tree, a little silent stranger grabbing at her and yanking her backward, their hot breath pressing against the nape of her neck.

She tried to scream, but before she had the chance, a hand clamped over her mouth, pressing something sharp against her neck.

And then everything faded to black.

2

One Month Later

A storm had settled like a curse over the quiet town of Cambria, the sky splitting open with sheets of rain that showed no signs of stopping. The wind howled low around the eaves, and every drop against my office window felt like a warning tap.

Something was coming.

I could feel it.

I was sitting at my desk when the front door blew open and a woman rushed in, umbrella in hand. She flicked the umbrella downward, scattering droplets of water across the wood floor. Then she pressed a button, collapsing it as she fastened the clasp around it.

Brushing off her damp gray trench coat, she scanned the room. When her gaze met mine, she walked over, offering a small smile as she stepped inside my office.

The woman was, in a word, disheveled. Her long, dirty-blond hair looked like it had once been tied in a bun, but the blustery weather had pulled it loose. She sank into the chair across from me, unbuttoned her coat, and slipped it off, revealing a cream-colored cashmere sweater.

She blinked at me and said, "Hello. I'm Rosemary Ashford."

I knew the name, and I knew her story.

Everyone in town did.

Her daughter, Audrey, had been murdered while walking through the woods to a friend's house, her throat cut from behind. The path she'd chosen that day was one she'd often traveled, a familiar trail turned fatal. Since then, whispers swept through town, talk of a killer on the loose, lurking in the woods, waiting to strike again.

Given no other attacks had happened since, I didn't buy it. Audrey's murder seemed deliberate and targeted, and it would surprise me to learn it wasn't.

"What can I do for you, Mrs. Ashford?" I asked.

"Call me Rosemary, please. I heard you used to be a detective for the San Luis Obispo Police Department, and a few years ago, you left to open your own detective agency."

"You heard right."

"I ... ahh ... I was hoping to talk to you about ..."

Before she could finish her sentence, the tears came, fast and hard like a sprinkler set to full blast. I opened one of my desk drawers and reached for a box of tissues, which I set in front of her.

"I'm sorry about what happened to Audrey," I said. "How's the police investigation going?"

"I'm not sure how long a murder investigation should take, but this one seems to be dragging," she admitted. "That's not to say the police haven't been thorough. They've kept me informed and have been in constant contact ever since my daughter died. Still, they don't have much in the way of leads yet."

She was right.

They didn't have any solid leads, not a single one.

None they'd shared with me, anyway.

"Chief Foley is my brother-in-law," I said. "He's married to my sister, Phoebe. And Whitlock, the lead detective, is a close family friend. I've spoken with both of them several times over the past few weeks, and I can assure you; they're putting everything they have into finding your daughter's killer and bringing them to justice."

She leaned back in her chair, letting out a frustrated sigh. "That may be true. Still, I'd like to hire you. I'm hoping that, with your help, things will move along faster."

Ever since the day I heard about Audrey's murder, I'd kept an eye on the case, touching base with Foley and Whitlock now and then, but since they hadn't sought out my advice, I'd kept my thoughts to myself. Until now, it hadn't been my place to interfere. That was all about to change.

For most murder investigations, I worked alongside my team—two women who, like me, came from law enforcement. Hunter had served as a detective in the same county I once did, while Simone had built her career as a forensic anthropologist. Shortly after I opened the detective agency, they both came on board. Since then, we'd operated as a tight unit whenever we took on a murder investigation. Hunter remained in the background, piecing together suspect intel, and Simone spoke to friends, neighbors, and potential suspects.

With the agency slowing down over the past two months, Hunter had gone to spend time with her sister, and Simone had taken off on a vacation with Paul—her husband, and my brother. Without them, the case would require a lot of extra work. Still, I felt steady and confident I could handle it on my own.

"I'll take the case," I said.

"Good. When can you start?"

"Now."

She pressed her hands together, pleased. "Is there anything you need from me?"

"I know some of the details about the investigation, but there's a lot I still don't know," I said. "Do you feel up to answering some questions?"

"Even if I'm not, I'll muddle my way through them."

I reached for the cup of tea I'd made myself earlier, but one sip told me it had already gone cold. I set it aside.

"What was Audrey's demeanor like in the weeks prior to her death?" I asked.

"Much the same as always, I suppose. My daughter was the quiet type, even around her father and me. She'd chat with us about everyday things, but when it came to her own feelings, she was often cautious about what she shared."

"Why do you think Audrey kept so much to herself?"

"She was an introvert. Been on the quiet side ever since she was a kid."

"Do you have any other children?"

She shook her head. "After Audrey was born, we tried to conceive again, but we were unable to have another child."

I imagined it made the sting of Audrey's death even more painful.

"What were Audrey's relationships like with her friends?" I asked.

Rosemary crossed one leg over the other. "She had plenty of acquaintances but not many close friends. I always described her friend groups as her outer and inner circles. Most stayed on the outer edge, but a few, like Talia Kinkaid, were trusted with the parts of Audrey that no one else saw.”

“How long had Audrey been friends with Talia?”

“Since they were four years old. They attended preschool together. Once they met, they became fast friends, and before we knew it, they were inseparable.” She paused, then added, “Talia’s parents have stopped by a few times since the funeral. They seem worried. They told me Talia doesn’t leave her room most days, and she hasn’t eaten much since Audrey died.”

Hearing about Talia’s close relationship with Audrey, I looked forward to speaking with her, and I hoped when I did she would be willing to talk.

“Was Audrey dating anyone before she died?”

Rosemary hesitated. “She was dating Logan. He lives across the street from us, and he’s known Audrey since grade school. I’d always suspected he liked her, but he’d never acted on it, not until a few months before she died. He turned up at our door with pink roses, a box of chocolates, and a poem he’d written about a teenager with a crush. It was the sweetest thing.”

“I wonder what pushed him to act on his feelings.”

“Oh, I know why he did it. A new boy moved to town, and he didn’t wait long before he showed an interest in Audrey.”

“What’s the new boy’s name?”

“Colton Jagger.”

“What did Audrey think of Colton?”

“She found him to be pushy and aggressive, though I doubt she ever told him to his face. She did send him a text message telling him the attention he was giving her was making her feel overwhelmed, and she thought they should just be friends.”

“How did he respond?”

“Not with any actual words, but he did send her a couple of emojis, an X and a thumbs-down.” Shaking her head, she added, "Teens these days. It's like no one knows how to communicate anymore."

"So, Audrey shot Colton down. What about Logan?"

"I assumed Audrey and Logan would date one day, and I was right. Once Logan made his feelings known, Audrey admitted she felt the same, and they started seeing each other."

In the short time she'd been there, Rosemary had provided me with two possible suspects, and we were just getting started. Conversations with grieving parents were always the hardest, and Rosemary was no exception. It never felt right to press, but I had questions, hard ones, and they couldn't go unasked.

"What can you tell me about the last day Audrey was alive?" I asked.

Rosemary gripped the chair as if steadying herself for the conversation ahead. "It was an ordinary day. She stayed in her room for most of it, sorting through closets and drawers, trying to choose what would go with her to college and what she'd donate to charity. It was almost dinnertime, and she came downstairs, letting me know she was heading over to Talia's house."

"Was the visit to Talia's planned or spontaneous?"

"Planned. They were going to talk about their college send-off party."

"What's a send-off party?"

"Talia, Audrey, and a few of their friends had booked a weekend away at an oceanfront house in Santa Barbara. It would have been the last chance for them all to be together before they left for college."

"What are the names of the other friends?"

She tapped a finger to her lips, thinking. "Let's see now ... I believe the other three were Willow Robinson, Sadie Holt, and

McKenna Moore. There might be a couple of others. I'm not sure."

"What time did Audrey leave for Talia's house?"

"Oh, about half past five."

"After sunset."

Rosemary nodded. "She'd wanted to head over earlier, but packing up her room took a lot longer than she thought it would."

"How often did Audrey cut through the woods?"

Rosemary gave it some thought. "I'd say more often than not. Talia's house isn't far, about a ten-minute walk from our place. We spoke in the kitchen for a few minutes, and then I told her to text me when she got there. She said she would, and that was the last ... the last time I ever ..."

The tears welled up again, and she reached for a fresh tissue, blotting her eyes and then pressing the tissue to her nose.

I waited.

It couldn't have been easy for her, sitting across from me, reliving the last moments she spent with her daughter.

A few minutes passed, and I said, "I know how hard this must be, dredging up the memories that are painful to think about. If it's too difficult, we can talk again later. I have enough to get started."

Rosemary shook her head and reached for some more tissues. "If it's all right, I'd like to finish."

"Of course."

She took a few deep breaths in and continued. "After Audrey left the house, I was busy cleaning up the kitchen. A half hour went by before I realized Audrey hadn't texted me to let me know she'd arrived at Talia's. I sent her a text, and when I didn't hear back, I called Brianne, Talia's mother. She said Audrey hadn't arrived yet, and that Talia had sent Audrey a text message but hadn't heard from her either. She figured Audrey must have gotten sidetracked and wasn't coming over."

"What did you do when you learned she never made it to Talia's house?"

"I ran into the living room, where my husband, Dustin, was watching television. I told him Audrey wasn't at Talia's. He threw on his coat, grabbed a flashlight, and went out to search for her. Minutes later he returned, his face drained of all color. The second he walked through the door, he fell to his knees, covering his face with his hands. Then he looked at me. He didn't need to utter a single word. In that moment, I knew something awful had happened."

3

"Why am I not surprised?"

Foley leaned back in his chair, laced his fingers behind his head, and sighed.

Whitlock laughed, nudging me with his elbow. "You should know ... we made a bet about how long it would take before you got involved in our case."

"Who won?" I asked.

"Neither of us. Foley said one week, and I said two. We didn't think you had it in you to restrain yourself for an entire month. No offense."

"I was trying to let you two do your jobs."

Foley cocked his head, raising a brow. "Since when? You've been in here every week since the girl's murder. Maybe you weren't running your own investigation, but you sure as hell angled for details."

"Can you blame me?"

"Suppose not. Word is your sidekicks are out of town. You planning to work the case without Hunter and Simone?"

I grinned and said, "They're not my *only* sidekicks, though, are they?"

Foley wagged a finger at me. "Oh, no. If you think we're your backup, you're mistaken. If anything, it's the other way around."

"I never asked you to help me. I'm here to help you."

"Help us *how*?"

"I haven't worked that part out yet. Why don't we start by you telling me what you know. And I'll ... well, I'll listen."

Foley snorted. "Listening isn't helping."

Maybe not, but it was a start.

"If you're done giving me grief, I'd like to know where you are on the case," I said.

"And if I'm not done?"

I shrugged. "Then I'll wait. I have time."

Foley glanced at Whitlock, and the two of them burst out laughing.

"All right, let's get to the case," Foley said. "What do you want to know?"

"Everything."

"Everything, huh? We want to know everything too, starting with what Rosemary Ashford told you."

"We talked about Audrey's friends and the guys who were interested in her, and then she walked me through the day Audrey died. She told me it was Dustin, Audrey's father, who found her."

"Yeah, that was rough," Whitlock said. "Poor guy."

"I feel for him," Foley added. "When he found her, he tried to pick her up, like he meant to carry her home. But his legs gave out, and he collapsed. The problem is, he moved her from the spot where she died. Disturbed the ground all around her. I don't blame him, but it sure would have been better if she hadn't been moved."

"Did you find anything at the scene, anything useful?" I asked, leaning forward in my chair.

"Not a thing. Her throat was slit, and if the killer left a knife behind, we'd have found it. We didn't."

Whitlock shifted in his seat, rubbing a hand along his jaw. "Crazy thing is, she almost made it to her friend's house. Couple more minutes, and she would've been there."

"I'm not familiar with that part of the woods," I said. "Anything I should know?"

"I'd say it's a wooded area that's not used all that often. About a five-minute walk from where we found Audrey, we came across a cabin. Well, the remains of what used to be a cabin. Old place. Needs to be torn down."

"How old are we talking?"

"Hundred years, maybe more. I dug into the records, tried to figure out who built it and who owned it last. Nothing. It's like the place doesn't exist on paper."

"Someone must know something about it."

"If they do, they're not talking," he said, his gaze fixed on me.

I paused, gearing up for my next question. "Do you have any suspects yet?"

"Everyone who knew that girl is a suspect. We just haven't tied the murder to anyone yet."

"Do you suspect one person over the rest?"

"We'll get to that in a minute. First, I want to circle back to the cabin and what we found there. For starters, it seems someone had been inside it in recent months."

"How do you know?"

"Place should have been crawling with cobwebs. It wasn't. Didn't see a single one."

"You think someone cleaned it up?"

"Seems so."

Whitlock, who hadn't been as talkative as usual, raised a

hand as if needing permission to speak. "And then there's the initials we found."

"*What* initials?"

"AA. Carved into one of the wooden beams."

My stomach tightened.

AA

Audrey Ashford.

She could have carved it herself—but why?

Was the old cabin a place she frequented, somewhere she could go to be alone with her thoughts? Or had it served a different purpose, one we weren't aware of yet?

"Who have you talked to so far?" I asked.

"Family, friends, classmates. You name it, we've spoken to them."

"Before, when I asked if there was someone you suspected over the rest, you didn't give me a definitive answer."

Foley and Whitlock exchanged glances, remaining silent.

Whatever detail they were keeping from me, it appeared to be a juicy one.

"All right, you two, what aren't you telling me?" I asked.

"Our main suspect is Logan Lambert," Foley said.

"The guy Audrey was dating? Why? Have you spoken to him?"

"We have."

"And?"

"He was nervous, more nervous than he should have been if he was innocent."

"Where was he at the time of Audrey's murder?"

"He said he was home alone. I spoke to his parents. They were out to dinner on the night of the murder. They said Logan was home when they went out that night and when they got back. But they were out for a couple of hours, and it just happened to coincide with the time the murder took place."

"It doesn't mean Logan's guilty of anything. Do you have any evidence to suggest otherwise?"

"Not yet."

"Then why is he your main suspect?"

"We dropped by his parents' house a few days ago to speak to him again. They said Logan had left town for the weekend with a couple of his friends, but we talked to those friends. They said they'd made no such plans."

"Why would Logan lie about it?"

"That's what we would like to know. I circled back to Logan's parents again this morning, hoping he was back so we could ask him a few more questions. But he wasn't around, which means no one's seen the kid in four days."

4

Four days earlier, a gas station security camera had caught Logan on surveillance. He rolled up to the pump, parked his truck, and climbed out, dressed in dark jeans and a black hoodie, the hood shadowing a baseball cap pulled low on his head.

Logan filled the tank, went inside, and piled a basket full of junk food and drinks. He returned to his truck minutes later and opened the passenger-side door. A duffel bag could be seen sitting on the floor. He set the food and drinks on top of it and then slid into the driver's seat.

It was the last time he'd been seen.

I parked in Logan's parents' driveway, and when I exited my vehicle, I was surprised to see Rosemary walking to the front door. She made a fist like she was preparing to knock, and then she hesitated and turned toward me.

"Hey, Georgiana, what are you doing here?" she asked.

"I came to speak with Logan's parents."

"Then I guess you heard."

"That Logan's missing? Yeah, I did."

Rosemary moved a hand to her hip. "I had no idea. My next-door neighbor just told me, and I came right over. I have to say, I'm worried. What if the man who killed Audrey has Logan? Or even worse, what if Logan's dead too?"

"Until we have more information, we shouldn't jump to any conclusions just yet," I said.

"It's hard not to, don't you think? Why else would he leave and not return home after a couple of days?"

"Logan told his parents he was going out of town for the weekend with friends. But when those friends were questioned, they said no plans had ever been made."

"It doesn't make sense. It's not like Logan to lie. He's a good kid. An honest one, too, in my experience."

Not completely honest, it seemed.

He'd lied to his parents.

But why?

Was it so they wouldn't worry?

Worrying was inevitable.

It was just a matter of time before they realized they'd been misinformed.

Foley seemed convinced Logan was their prime suspect. He didn't say it right out, but I could tell. Maybe I should have leaned into that possibility more myself. After all, the young man was on the run. But before I condemned him, I needed to know more, and I needed proof, evidence suggesting he played a role in Audrey's death.

I knocked on the door, and it swung open to reveal a middle-aged woman with short, curly red hair and striking blue eyes. Clad in yoga gear and a bit out of breath, she looked at us as though we'd interrupted her usual workout.

The woman looked at Rosemary, then at me. "Who are you? And why are the two of you carrying on outside my front door?"

Rosemary tipped her head my way. "Tilly, this is Georgiana Germaine. She's a private detective. It's been a month since

Audrey died, and I thought the police might need a little extra help, so I've hired her to investigate."

A gust of cool air swept past, and I seized the folds of my black velvet coat, a 1920s relic with puffed sleeves, pulling it snug against myself. "Would it be all right if I come in and ask you a few questions?"

Tilly frowned. "I'd rather you didn't."

It wasn't the response I was hoping for, and I paused a moment, trying to come up with a different approach.

"I just need a few minutes of your time," I said. "If your son is missing, I can help find him."

She flung her hands in the air, exhaling a frustrated sigh. "Why does everyone *assume* my son is missing?"

"From what I understand, Logan told you and your husband he was going away with friends. The police spoke to those friends. They said no plans were ever made."

"He didn't tell *me* he was going away with friends. He told his father, Vaughn. I'm not sure what all the fuss is about. I'm sure he's fine. He's a resourceful kid, always has been."

Spoken like a mother who would say anything to protect her son.

"Have you heard from Logan since he left?" I asked.

"No."

"It's been four days. Aren't you worried?"

Tilly cast a quick look behind her, scanning the hall as though she was concerned someone might overhear our conversation, and then she looked at me. "When Logan gets overwhelmed, he takes off sometimes."

I wasn't buying it, but I decided to play along, for now.

"When he disappears like that, how long does he stay away?" I asked.

She shrugged. "Until he feels like coming home."

Rosemary raised a brow, a silent gesture that told me she

wasn't fond of Tilly's answer. "I must say, I've never known Logan to take off this way."

Tilly cast Rosemary a sharp look, a silent warning to hold her tongue, but Rosemary wasn't having it.

"I'd like you to explain to me why you won't accept Georgiana's help," Rosemary said. "Your son is missing. Have you ever considered he might be in some kind of trouble?"

Tilly leaned back, crossing her arms. "I'm sure he's fine."

"But what if he *isn't* fine?"

They squared off, and Tilly's nostrils flared. She reached out, attempting to slam the door in our faces, but I jammed my boot inside just in time to stop her.

"How dare you!" Tilly fumed. "Even if I knew where my son was, I wouldn't tell you. I'm sorry for what you're going through, Rosemary. But I want you to leave. Both of you. Now."

"I'll leave as soon as you stop lying to me," I said. "And don't bother trying to defend yourself. Your breathing has changed, becoming faster and shallower the longer we talk, and your responses sound rehearsed. Ever since I introduced myself, you haven't met my eyes once. All classic tells. You're either hiding something from me or you're lying to me. Or maybe a bit of both."

Tilly glanced down the hallway again. This time, a man walked toward her, and she squeezed her eyes shut, as though wishing he hadn't become aware of our conversation.

The man said a quick hello to Rosemary, and then he turned toward Tilly. "Everything okay here?"

"No, Vaughn," Tilly said. "Everything is *not* okay. This woman is Georgiana Germany, and she—"

"It's Germaine," I corrected.

"Germany, Germaine, whatever. Anyway, Rosemary hired her to investigate Audrey's murder."

Vaughn clapped his hands together. "That's wonderful

news, isn't it? The sooner we get answers, the sooner her family can find the peace they all deserve."

"It may be wonderful news for Rosemary, but it it's not so wonderful for us."

He narrowed his eyes. "What do you mean?"

"Georgiana came here to press us for information about Logan."

Vaughn tapped a finger to the door, thinking. Then he said, "I'd like to speak to the detective alone."

"What?" Tilly said. "No—why?"

He placed a hand on his wife's shoulder, giving it a squeeze. "Trust me, honey. It's best I speak with her. All right?"

"I don't understand."

Rosemary stepped into the Lamberts' house as if she owned the place, looped her arm in Tilly's and said, "Come on, friend. Let's have a drink. What do you say?"

With a great deal of reluctance, Tilly nodded, and they disappeared down the hall.

And then there were two.

5

"I was thinking perhaps we could speak in private," Vaughn said.

Given our lack of privacy options, I suggested we go for a drive. He agreed, and we were off. As soon as we pulled out of the driveway, I said, "Why did you want to speak to me alone?"

"I need to admit something to you," he said. "I lied."

"About what?"

"My son."

"What about him?"

"When the chief of police came to see me, I wasn't prepared for their questions. At the time, Logan hadn't even been gone for a day, so my wife didn't think anything about the fact that he hadn't returned home yet. Chief Foley was determined to speak to Logan So, not wanting to alarm my wife, I said he'd left for the weekend with friends."

"Was it something you made up, or was it what Logan told you?"

"I made it up. And look, I'm not a dishonest person."

"Why did you lie, then?"

"I was trying to spare my wife. She's been stressed about Logan's wellbeing ever since Audrey died. I was hoping to find my son before anyone knew he hadn't come home yet. And then the police showed up. I had to make a snap decision, and I did."

"Lying to the police is never the right decision."

"I get that, which is why I'm telling you now. I have every intention of going to the police department later to explain."

"When you say 'later,' how much later?"

"Today, all right?"

"I'll give you until the end of the day, and if you haven't told them by then, I will. I appreciate the honesty, but you never should have kept it to yourself for this long. Your son has been on the run for four days."

"I wouldn't say he's 'on the run.'"

"Then what would you call it?"

"He's processing Audrey's death, and he's not ready to talk to anyone—not the police, not you, not even his own parents. He's a teenager, it's what they do. He just needs a little time. That's all."

I pulled into a parking lot, the car idling as I continued questioning him.

"Have you had any interaction with your son since he left?" I asked.

He squirmed in his seat, uneasy.

"Well ...?" I pressed. "Have you spoken to him or not?"

He sighed. "Once."

"When?"

"The day he left."

"What did he say?"

"We didn't talk long. He said he needed to take some time to himself, and he told me he didn't want his mother to worry. I assured him I'd think of something to tell her, but I warned him if he stayed away too long she'd start to get suspicious."

"How did the call end?"

"I told him to be safe and that I was here for him if he needed me."

"Doesn't it worry you that he hasn't come back yet?"

Vaughn turned, staring out the window at nothing in particular. "If he's not back in a few more days, I will be. He's a resourceful, capable kid. Always has been. He loves going camping by himself, which is what I expect he's been doing. Helps him clear his head when he has a lot on his mind."

It struck me as odd that both parents were being so aloof about their missing child. If it had been my child, no matter the age or how capable I found them to be, I'd be worried.

"What was Logan's demeanor like before he left?" I asked.

"A lot quieter than usual. He's been a bit depressed and moping around a lot. I figure it will take some time for him to process all that's happened. I suggested he speak to a therapist about what's happened, but he had no interest."

"I'd like to have a look at his room."

"I'm not comfortable with that, and my wife won't be either."

It was the answer I'd expected, but it was worth a try.

Switching gears, I said, "I hear you went out to dinner with your wife the night Audrey died. Where'd you go?"

"Nothing too fancy. The Boathouse Diner."

"It may not be fancy, but the food's good."

He patted down his pant pockets, then looked at me, a nervous expression on his face.

"What is it?" I asked.

"My phone. I must have left it at the house. What time is it?"

I pointed at the clock on the dash.

He shook his head, saying, "I didn't realize we'd been gone this long. I need to get home. My wife will be waiting."

"Why? Do you two have plans?"

"Tilly has an old college roommate in town. We're going out for a couple of drinks."

There it was again, Vaughn carrying on as if his son not returning home was nothing out of the ordinary, but it did give me an idea.

Vaughn and Tilly weren't the only ones with plans.

I had plans of my own.

Plans to do a little sneaking around.

6

The sun hung low in the sky, melting into the horizon in a wash of amber and violet. In another thirty minutes, the neighborhood would be cloaked in darkness, giving me the perfect opportunity to get in and out of Logan's parents' house without being seen.

From my vantage point, the house sat quiet, appearing uninhabited. Vaughn's car was no longer in the driveway, which told me they'd left to meet up with Tilly's college roommate. Still, I needed to be sure.

Checking my phone for the time, I confirmed it wouldn't be long before dusk would give me the cover I needed to cross the street and make my way inside their house and into Logan's room. It was the one place I hoped to find clues about Audrey's death and provide me with answers about why Logan left town and hadn't returned.

As the last bit of light faded over the horizon, I crossed the street, opening the side gate into the back yard. Walking up the wooden porch steps, one of them creaked, something I hadn't expected. I stopped and listened, glancing around to see if any neighbors were around. I heard nothing and saw no one, and I approached the sliding glass door. Getting in was easier than I'd expected; the door had been left unlocked. I slipped inside and shut the door behind me, taking in the faint aroma of lemon cleaner and something else—a hint of vanilla.

To make sure Vaughn and Tilly were out for the evening, and I was all alone in the house, I cupped a hand to the side of my mouth and shouted, "Hello? Is anyone here?"

I was met with silence.

I called out once more and was met with the same, giving me the all-clear to continue with my plan.

Moving through the kitchen, I caught sight of the living room curtains at the front of the house. They were drawn, so I pulled the mini flashlight I always carried out of my purse. I clicked it on and scanned the room. On the opposite side, a table was set with plates and silverware, as if waiting for the family to sit down for dinner. Maybe it was always arranged that way—for appearances, if nothing else.

I walked to a bookcase, peering down at a photograph of Logan in his cap and gown, his parents at his side, beaming with pride.

They looked happy, so put together.

But were they?

Or was it an illusion, a way to make everything seem perfect when it wasn't?

I found the stairs and took them one at a time until I reached the top. Logan's room was at the end of the hall, his door half open when I got to it. A faint smell of cologne lingered in the air. I stepped inside, allowing time for my eyes to adjust. Beside Logan's bed was a wooden desk. On top of it were tin cans filled with colored pencils. Given the wall was lined with colored sketches, drawing appeared to be one of his hobbies.

I continued to search the room and spotted an easel near the window. The sketch attached to it stopped me cold. It was a woman's face, unfinished, and ghostly, drawn in graphite. The features were unmistakable. Audrey's likeness stared back at me, captured with an intimacy that made my stomach twist.

I wondered when he'd drawn it.

Before she died, when she was still full of life?

Or after, when guilt and grief had driven him to preserve her memory in lead and paper?

I snapped a photo of the drawing and continued to look around. Shifting my attention back to the desk, I saw a series of notebooks next to the pencil cans. I grabbed one of them and began to flip through its pages. Each drawing seemed to tell a story, small fragments of a life pieced together in colored pencil. Some of the drawings were of ordinary things like coffee cups, street corners, and a dog sleeping by the fire. Others appeared much more personal. I felt like I was walking through his memories, each page representing a moment in time he'd captured so he wouldn't forget.

I set the notebook back down and rested my hand on the edge of the desk. And that's when I felt it, something that didn't belong, a texture that was different, smoother than the rest of the wood. I crouched down and aimed the beam of my flashlight under the desk. There, taped to the underside, was another notebook. It looked identical to the others, but the fact that it had been hidden told me something about it was different.

Flipping it open, the first few pages were filled with sketches of a wooded landscape and trees leaning toward a narrow creek, the kind of place where the air smelled of moss and rain. I couldn't tell if Logan had drawn it from a memory, but the detail suggested the place mattered to him. I turned another page, and the tone of the drawings changed. The woods gave way to something smaller and more personal—a locket. The locket was silver and oval in shape, and along the outer edge was a delicate ring of hearts. At its center was a name: *Anne.*

I flipped to the next page and found the same locket staring back at me, only the second version was a lot more refined. I turned another page, then another, my pulse quickening, hoping for something that might explain why he'd sketched the locket in the first place. But the pages ahead were empty.

I snapped the sketchbook closed and slid it into my purse, my mind filled with questions.

Was the locket real and had it belonged to someone?

Or was it something he'd imagined?

If it was real, was Anne real, someone he knew?

If so, why would Logan do renderings of Anne's locket when he was in a relationship with Audrey?

As I pondered those thoughts, I heard what sounded like a car door closing outside. I froze, contemplating my options. After a short pause, I heard heavy footsteps, followed by someone whistling.

There was a knock at the front door, which gave me a moment of relief. If Logan's parents had returned home, they wouldn't have knocked.

But if it wasn't them, who was it?

A minute passed, and I heard what sounded like someone walking away. I hurried down the stairs and out the back door. My plan was to wait until the unknown visitor started their vehicle and drove away, and then I'd make my escape. A few minutes later, a car whirred past. Thinking the visitor had left the premisis, I cut through the yard and reached the gate, easing it open. I hadn't taken more than a few steps before someone said, "Evening, Georgiana."

I jerked my head around and saw Whitlock with his hands in his pockets, one eyebrow lifted as he offered me a slight grin. Given his usual chatty demeanor, I thought he might say something more. But he didn't. He crossed his arms as if waiting for me to explain myself.

So I did.

Or I tried to ... "I was just ahh ... ahh ..."

"Somewhere you're not supposed to be, I'd say," he said. "I'm guessing the Lamberts are not at home."

"They're not. They're meeting up with one of Tilly's college friends."

"You want to tell me why you were sneaking around their backyard?"

It appeared he didn't know I'd been inside the house, and as I considered what to say and how much to say, I wasn't sure about the best way forward. I'd always had a good working relationship with Whitlock, and he was aware I sometimes bent the rules when I had to, something he couldn't do as a county detective. Lying to him, even a little bit, didn't seem right. And even if I did, there was a good chance he'd know it, which would make things even worse.

Honesty it is, then.

"I stopped by earlier today to speak to Tilly and Vaughn about Logan," I said. "I asked Vaughn if I could see Logan's room. He said no."

"So you decided to wait until they weren't home and to have a look anyway."

"Something like that."

"Are you aware this counts as breaking and entering?"

"I didn't break anything, and the back door was unlocked," I smirked. "To me, that's just entering."

He stared at me for a moment, then grinned. "You find anything?"

"Maybe, but before I give you all the details, did Logan's father contact you or Foley today?"

"No, why?"

"I need to talk to you about a conversation I had with him."

"All right. What was it about?"

"When you first questioned him, he told you that his son had told him he was going away for the weekend with friends."

Whitlock shrugged. "I know. We spoke about it earlier when you stopped by the department. What about it?"

I held his gaze and said, "The dad lied."

7

I sat in my den, a glass of pinot noir in hand. Across from me, Whitlock nursed a tumbler of whisky, his thumb tracing the rim before taking another sip. From the kitchen I could hear the steady rhythm of Giovanni at work, cooking up dinner, filet mignon for three.

Earlier, when I'd arrived home with Whitlock in tow, Giovanni had insisted the detective stay for dinner, saying, "There's no reason to discuss the case on an empty stomach when we can do it over dinner."

I agreed.

So did Whitlock, who quipped that he would never turn down a good steak, or Giovanni's cooking.

As we sat in the living room waiting for dinner to be ready, my attention turned to the logs in the fireplace, cracking and groaning as soft shadows danced across the opposite wall.

Whitlock took another sip of whisky, shot me a wink, and said, "Can't say I'm used to being invited to dinner by people I catch sneaking out of a house."

"It wouldn't be the first time."

He raised his glass, grinning at me as he said, "And I have no doubt it won't be the last."

We both laughed, and when it subsided, he redirected the conversation.

"How about we chat about Vaughn, and the lie you say he told."

I took another sip of wine, setting the glass down beside me. "Logan never told Vaughn he was going away for the weekend with friends. Vaughn made it up."

"Any idea why?"

"He said he was protecting his wife, making sure she didn't worry about Logan not coming home. He told me he planned to come to the department and explain everything to you, but since he hasn't, I'm not convinced he'll do it."

Whitlock leaned back, crossing one leg over the other. "Did Vaughn even have a conversation with Logan before the kid left?"

"Not before he left, but after. Vaughn said Logan called him to say he needed some time to himself. He told Logan not to worry."

"Was anything else said during the call?"

"If it was, Vaughn didn't say. He did mention that he'd told Logan not to stay away too long because his mother would get suspicious about why he hadn't returned home."

"By now, Logan must know his parents are worried."

"If they are, they're not acting like it. Not to me."

Whitlock shrugged. "Maybe they're worried and putting on a brave face so you and everyone else think everything is fine."

"Maybe."

Giovanni entered the room with Luka at his side, the robust scent of seared meat trailing in behind them. He picked up Whitlock's glass, topping it off with a generous pour of whisky.

"Dinner's ready," he said, handing the glass back to him.

"Too much more of this stuff, and I won't be able to drive home," Whitlock said.

"What's the rush?" Giovanni asked. "It's not every day I get to enjoy your company."

Whitlock smiled, and we rose from our chairs, making our way to the table.

As I took my seat, Whitlock jabbed a thumb in my direction. "This one doesn't know how to take no for an answer. Then again, she never did."

Giovanni raised a brow, a look of suspicion on his face. "What's she done this time?"

"Broke into a suspect's parents' house while they were out to get a peek inside their kid's bedroom."

"Like I said before, there was no *breaking* involved," I said.

Giovanni grinned and passed a serving platter filled with grilled vegetables. "And? Did you find anything worth the risk?"

"Funny," I said, cutting into my steak. "Whitlock asked me the same thing. And yes, I believe I did."

Both men paused mid-bite, knives resting on their plates, their attention shifting to me in perfect unison.

"Well ...?" Whitlock asked. "Let's have it then."

"The first thing I noticed when I walked into Logan's room was a half-sketched drawing of Audrey on an easel by his window. I didn't think much about it, although I have been wondering whether he'd started the sketch before or after she died."

"Does it matter?"

"Maybe not, but sometimes the simplest clues lead to the biggest discoveries. After I saw the sketch, I turned my attention to Logan's desk. Cans of colored pencils sat beside several notebooks filled with drawings. I flipped through them, but nothing struck me as unusual."

"What did you find that was worth the risk?" Giovanni asked.

"I'll tell you, but can we finish dinner first?"

"Sure."

I took my time eating, savoring my steak, and soon realized both men had wolfed theirs down, as if trying to rush so we could get to my discovery.

"All right, all right," I said. "I see what's going on here, you two."

"I don't know what you mean," Whitlock said with a wink.

"Yes, you do. You're both dying to know what I found."

I pushed my chair back and stood.

"Finish your dinner, *cara mia*," Giovanni said. "We can wait."

They could, but I got the feeling it would be a huge test of patience to make them wait while I finished my dinner.

I stood and walked to the den, reaching for my vintage Chanel bag. I grabbed the notebook out of it and returned to the table, slapping it down in front of them.

"You took this from Logan's room?" Whitlock asked.

"Sure did. And guess where I found it? Taped beneath his desk. He was hiding it. The question is—why?"

"Do you have any answers?"

"I might."

I opened the notebook and pointed. "This first drawing is interesting, but as to whether the place is real or imaginary, I don't recognize it. Do either of you?"

Both men shook their heads.

"Look at this," I said, flipping a few pages. "Logan started drawing a locket, and he even added a name, *Anne*."

"Interesting," Whitlock said.

"Why would he inscribe the locket with the name Anne if he

was in a relationship with Audrey?" I asked. "And if the name is of no significance, why include it?"

"Good questions."

Giovanni leaned in, taking a closer look. "Is this the only rendering of the locket?"

"There's one more." I flipped to the next page. "On this second one, he's added a lot more detail."

"I see."

"I wish I could say there's more, but this is the last entry in the notebook." I paused, then added, "The other notebook on Logan's desk is filled with drawings from the first page to the last. Since this one wasn't finished, I figured it was the most recent one he'd been using."

Whitlock set his plate to the side, crossing his arms in front of him. "You think this Anne person exists?"

"I do," I said. "And if we can figure out who she is, maybe we'll understand why he sketched the locket."

8

Morning sunlight filtered through a thin veil of mist that was spreading its way across town. I pulled my car to the side of a narrow road and looked around. The neighborhood was quiet, the kind of stillness that came before the day was off and running.

Talia's parents' cabin sat at the end of the lane, a modest cedar-sided place with a pitched green roof and a single step leading to the front door. Smoke drifted out of the top of the chimney, carrying the scent of burnt oak through the cool air.

I killed the engine and sat for a moment, listening to the birds chirping overhead, and I wished I'd brought my binoculars. But today, birdwatching wasn't on the agenda.

Sliding out of the car, the gravel in the driveway crunched under my boots as I started for the house, noting the front curtains were closed. I hoped I wasn't too early and that Talia would be in the mood to talk.

I stood on the front porch and knocked, unsure what kind of welcome I'd find. The door creaked open, and a man came into view. He was broad-shouldered, middle-aged, and had silver streaks running through his thick, dark hair. His flannel shirt looked well worn, the kind that had seen more than a few winters, and he was wearing jeans that were faded at the knees.

He gave me a polite nod and said, "Hi, can I help you?"

"I hope so. I'm Georgiana Germaine. I'm a private investigator, and I've been hired by Audrey's mother to help solve her murder."

"I see. It's good to meet you. I'm Gabriel."

"I was hoping I could speak with Talia."

He crossed his arms, tipping his head to the side. "You can try, but she hasn't been in much of a talking mood these past few weeks."

"I get it. She lost a good friend."

"A great friend. The two of them had been attached at the hip since elementary school."

I nodded, and for a moment, the silence between us felt heavy until it was broken by the tick of a clock somewhere deeper in the cabin. Gabriel stepped back, motioning me inside, his eyes shifting toward the hallway before returning to me.

Voice lowered, he said, "Talia hasn't been herself since Audrey died. I wish we could find a way to get through to her, but so far, nothing we've tried seems to be working."

"You'll find a way. She just needs time."

I followed Gabriel down a short hallway that opened into a kitchen. The scent of coffee and butter hung thick in the air, and at the stove I saw a woman with soft curls of blond hair and an apron tied over a gray tracksuit.

Upon hearing us enter the room, she turned, spatula in hand.

"Oh, hello," she said, her eyes darting from Gabriel to me.

"This is Georgiana Germaine," Gabriel said. "She's a private investigator."

The woman's expression faded to sadness.

"Of course. Rosemary told me all about you." She wiped her

hands on her apron and came around the counter. "I'm Brianne. Audrey was like family to us. Talia adored her. We all did."

"I was sorry to hear what happened," I said. "I know how close they were."

Brianne pressed her lips together and nodded, blinking back the emotion welling in her eyes. "It doesn't seem real, you know? Last month she was here, sitting right at that table, talking to me about how she wanted to surprise Talia with something for her birthday. But she died before she could … before it ever …"

Gabriel approached his wife, placing a hand on her shoulder. "It's all right, honey."

"No, it isn't."

She turned, shifting her focus back to the breakfast she was cooking—scrambled eggs, potatoes, bacon. Switching the burner off, she faced me. "You should stay for breakfast, Georgiana. There's plenty."

"I appreciate the offer," I said. "It looks delicious. I've already eaten breakfast, but if it's not too much trouble, I'd appreciate a cup of coffee."

"Of course."

Gabriel gave his wife a squeeze, then said, "Let me see if Talia's up for company, or if she's up at all today."

He left the room, his footsteps fading down the hall as Brianne handed me a cup of coffee. She dished up three plates of food and said, "Talia hasn't been coming down for breakfast. Every day I wake up and think, *Maybe today will be different.*"

"Your husband says she's been spending a lot of time in her room."

"She has, just listening to music and watching television most of the day. We've been trying to get through to her, to help her during this difficult time, but as a parent, it's hard to know what the right thing to do is in this unthinkable situation."

My thoughts drifted back to months earlier when I'd lost my best friend, and then further still, to the day I lost my daughter. I understood better than most what it meant to want nothing more than to disappear from the world. I'd done it myself—vanished without a trace after my daughter died, living off the grid for two years because I couldn't bear to face anyone or anything that reminded me of what I'd lost.

Grief changed people.

And for some, it was harder to bounce back than others.

"Everyone grieves in their own time," I said. "It isn't easy, but you take it one day at a time until you reach a point where the pain eases, even if only a little."

"You say it like you know a little something about it."

"I do, and if there's one piece of advice I could give you, it would be to say that your daughter is aware of the support you and your husband are trying to give her. I have no doubt she'll come through this when she's ready."

"How long did it take you, if you don't mind me asking?"

"Longer than it should have, but I'm in a different place now. I'd like to believe that, one day, your daughter will be too."

Gabriel reappeared in the doorway, his expression grim.

"I'm sorry," he said. "She's not up for visitors today."

"Well, I guess we ought to take her breakfast up to her then, before it gets cold," Brianne said. "Georgiana, you're welcome to join us at the table. Our daughter may not be up for a conversation, but perhaps we could be of some help."

"I'd like that," I said. "But first, would you mind if I took the plate of food up to Talia? I give you my word I won't press her with questions or do anything to make her uncomfortable."

They exchanged glances and though reluctant, Gabriel nodded, handing the plate of food over to me.

"Upstairs, first door on the left," Gabriel said.

I climbed the stairs, the old wood creaking underfoot as I

went. I reached Talia's bedroom door and paused, thinking about what to say when I saw her. As I mulled things over, I found myself staring at her bedroom door. The paint around the frame was chipped, and a faint trace of old stickers was still visible beneath a layer of dull white.

I knocked once, and the door eased open on its own, creaking just enough to let her know I was there. Inside, Talia sat cross-legged on her bed, lost in whatever world poured through her earbuds, as her head bobbed to its rhythm.

Her black plaid skirt was frayed at the hem and layered over torn fishnets, and she wore a blue shirt, which matched the color of her hair. She didn't seem to see me in the doorway, so I stepped inside, the faint scent of incense and nail polish drifting through the air as I entered.

Talia flinched, her head snapping up in surprise, and I lifted the plate toward her, hoping it would be enough to keep me from being thrown out before I even had the chance to speak.

She jerked the earbuds out of her ears, grabbed the plate, and said, "I told my dad I didn't want to talk to anyone."

"I know. I'm just here to bring you this plate of food."

She raised a brow, looking at me as if she wasn't buying it.

Glancing around, my eyes fell upon her record collection.

"I collect records too," I said.

This seemed to interest her.

"Oh, yeah?" she said. "What are you into?"

"Depends on the mood I'm in, I guess. One day it's Duran Duran, and the next it's Louis Armstrong. Louis was a famous—"

She lifted a finger, stopping me, set the plate on the nightstand, and hopped off the bed. She bent down and flipped through her record collection. She found the one she wanted and pulled it out, turning it over to show me.

"*Wonderful World, The Best of Louis Armstrong,*" I said. "I own it."

"This is an original."

"So's mine. I much prefer the original to a copy."

"Me too."

"My grandfather used to sing Louis Armstrong songs to me when I was little. I suppose it's how my love for jazz music got started."

She nodded, slipped the record into place on the turntable. The needle dropped, and the room filled with the warm crackle of vinyl as the sound of Louis' trumpet came in, bright and brassy, his voice rough with heart. Talia plopped back on the bed, eyeing me like she wondered why I was still standing there.

"Well, I'll leave you to eat your breakfast," I said.

"I doubt I'll eat any of it. My stomach's not good most days."

"I'm sorry about your friend."

"Sorry won't change anything. But hey, thanks."

On my way out, I turned. "I lost my best friend several months ago."

Talia folded her arms, leaning against the headrest as she said, "Oh, yeah? What happened?"

"There's no easy way to say this, so I'm just going to give it to you straight. She was murdered on my wedding day."

"Are you serious?"

I nodded. "I wish I wasn't. I caught the guy who did it, and though he'll spend the rest of his life in prison, it doesn't seem like it's enough. She died, and he's still living, even if the life he's living is behind bars. It's still a life or some semblance of one. Doesn't seem fair, does it?"

She reached for a piece of toast and took a bite, surprising me. "If I ask you a question, will you give me an honest answer?"

"Try me."

"If you could have killed the guy who murdered your friend and you were able to get away with it, would you have?"

The answer came right to me, though I hesitated before giving it.

"I have been put into positions many times when I've had to make a choice, and this one was one of the hardest. But yeah, I think some people deserve to die."

"Wow, that's dark. I like it."

"Listen, your father said you didn't feel up to talking to me about what happened, and I get it. All I ask is that when you are ready, you'll reach out to me, okay?"

"Yeah, okay."

I closed her bedroom door behind me and made my way downstairs. In the kitchen, the smell of coffee lingered as I joined Talia's parents at the table. Brianne sat with her hands wrapped around a mug, staring into it as though lost in thought, while Gabriel tried to fill the silence with polite conversation about the weather, the neighborhood, anything but the obvious.

We talked for a few minutes, and then a soft creak came from the stairwell. I glanced over my shoulder and caught sight of Talia standing on the bottom step, one hand gripping the banister. Her bright blue hair fell forward, shadowing her face as she hovered there, hesitant but listening to our conversation.

Gabriel noticed her standing there and said, "Hey, honey, do you want to join us?"

"I ... no." Then she looked at me. "Hey, Georgiana, do you want to go for a walk?"

9

The morning's light had softened by the time we set out, but the air was still cool enough to see our breaths when we spoke. The forest behind the neighborhood seemed to stretch on for miles, a dense weave of pine and oak that swallowed sound the deeper we went.

Talia walked beside me, her hands buried in the pockets of her oversized jacket, her headphones looped around her neck instead of in her ears. The blue in her hair caught the light like streaks of sapphire each time the wind kicked up.

She pushed a pair of sunglasses over the ridge of her nose and said, "Do you mind if we just walk for a minute?"

I nodded, taking what she'd said as her way of asking whether we could skip the talking for now. Considering she hadn't planned to speak to me at all when I showed up at the house, it felt like progress. Maybe, if I gave her time, she'd change her mind.

We followed a narrow trail that wound through the trees, past a patch of moss-covered stones and a half-collapsed fence that once marked someone's property line. The smell of damp earth filled the air, mingling with the faint sweetness of pine needles. When we reached a small clearing, I could almost picture how it must have looked that night when Audrey had left for Talia's house, unaware she was being followed.

Talia stopped beside a fallen log, her gaze fixed on the forest floor. "This is where they found her. It's crazy, you know? I look around, and it's like nothing ever happened here. But for me, I feel frozen in place. Weeks have passed, but I'm still stuck right here, and I can't seem to move on from it."

"There's no rush, no timeline on grieving."

"I feel like a different person, like the person I was when she was alive died with her, even though I'm still here."

I turned toward her. "I know what you mean. When you lose someone like that, it changes everything—how you see the world, how you see yourself. It's like you're still breathing, still moving through the same spaces, but part of you stayed behind with them. I've felt that too."

She paused, then said, "Whoa, that's deep."

"I get the feeling you're a deep person, an old soul like me. Am I right?"

She nodded.

"Talia, I know you're struggling to talk about Audrey, but since you asked me to go for a walk with you, I was hoping I could ask you about a few things. It would be a big help. If you're not ready though, I get it."

She took a breath, steadying herself. "How long have you been a private investigator?"

"Let's see, about four years now. Before that, I was a detective for the San Luis Obispo County."

"Have you ... uhh, solved many murders?"

"Twelve in the past five years."

"Twelve out of how many?"

She was testing me, but it kept the conversation going, which gave me hope.

"It might be easier if I said there's never been a murder case I've worked on that I *haven't* solved."

"Are you serious?"

"Sure am."

"What do you want to ask me?"

It seemed my patience was about to pay off.

"In the days before Audrey's death, what was she like?" I asked.

Talia glanced toward the trees. "Quieter than usual. I could tell something was off, but every time I asked, she brushed it off, told me not to worry. Which, of course, made me worry even more."

"Do you have any idea what it might've been?"

She shook her head. "None."

"What about Logan? How were they doing?"

Talia gave a small snort and rolled her eyes. "Annoying."

"How so?"

"There was this party one night. Every time I left for a minute, I'd come back and find them whispering somewhere off to the side. The second I walked up, they'd go quiet, pretend they'd been talking about something else. But I knew better."

"Any idea what they were talking about?"

"No, but I'd been friends with Audrey almost my whole life. I could always tell when she was hiding something from me."

"Why do you think she was talking to Logan about whatever it was, but not to you?"

Talia sighed and pushed her hands into her jacket pockets. "Earlier that week, she saw me hanging out with Colton."

"Colton Jagger? The new guy?"

"You know about him?"

"I heard he liked Audrey," I said.

"He did," she replied. "But she thought he was pushy, and she wanted nothing to do with him. I didn't see him that way, though. Once I got to know him, I mean yeah, he's a little immature sometimes, but it's not a big deal. Audrey didn't like that we were spending time together. She said it was weird because she and I were friends, and he liked her first."

"Do you think your friendship with Colton had something to do with the way she'd been acting around you?"

"Maybe. Even if it did, though, we'd made a pact in middle school. We were friends first, no matter what. Nothing was supposed to come between us." She paused, her voice tightening. "But I mean, maybe Colton had something to do with the way she was acting. Hard to say."

"What about your other friends at school?" I asked. "Any problems there?"

Talia thought for a moment. "At that same party, our friend Sadie had too much to drink. One of our other friends offered to drive her home, and after they left, Audrey noticed Sadie had forgotten her purse. She texted her and said she'd hang on to it for her."

"Seems like a kind thing for a friend to do," I said.

"That was Audrey. Always looking out for everyone. The next day, Sadie showed up to get her bag. Later that afternoon, she started blowing up Audrey's phone, accusing her of stealing money. Said a couple hundred dollars was missing."

"She accused Audrey of taking it?" I asked.

"She did. Right away too. Audrey was furious, and she called me, crying. I told her I'd handle it." Talia brushed a strand of hair off her face. "None of us knew how long Sadie's purse had been sitting on the counter before Audrey found it. The house was packed with people that night. Anyone could have taken the money."

"When you tried to reason with Sadie, did it work?"

"She backed off, but things weren't the same after that. We'd been planning a girls' trip before college—me, Audrey,

Sadie, and two others—but after the argument, Audrey said she didn't want Sadie to come with us. Said she couldn't trust her anymore."

"That must've made things awkward."

"It did. Audrey was planning to talk to me about it that night, the night she … you know … died."

Her voice faltered, and she went quiet.

"Was Sadie aware of how Audrey felt?" I asked.

"Oh, yeah," Talia said, her tone flat. "Sadie knew. Everyone in our friend group did, and then somehow it started getting around, and some of our friends started throwing shade at Sadie. They couldn't believe she'd accuse Audrey, of all people, of stealing from her."

"How did Audrey feel once it got around?"

"Audrey kept things to herself. She preferred peace and avoided anything that caused drama." She paused, then added, "I've come out here a few times, hoping to, I don't know, connect with Audrey somehow. I guess I thought being in the place where she was last alive might make me feel closer to her. Weird, huh?"

"Not at all. I visit some of my loved ones who've passed at the cemetery, and I talk to them. I find it's a good way to get some of my feelings out when I'm having a hard time or being challenged by something I can't figure out on a case."

"When you do that, do you feel closer to them?"

"Most of the time, yeah. What about you?"

"Sometimes I feel her, like she's standing right beside me, even though no one is there."

"Do you ever worry about coming out here? Whoever killed Audrey could be anywhere."

She reached into her pocket and pulled out a small pocketknife, turning it over in her hand before pressing the button on the side. The blade flicked open with a sharp click.

"I keep this with me," she said, her grip tightening on the handle. "People think I'm fragile, that I can't handle what happened. But they're wrong. I'm not afraid, and I want to look the person who took her life in the eye. I want them to know what they took from me."

The knife's blade caught the light, and I felt a knot tighten in my chest. "I understand why you feel that way. You want justice, and I respect that. But confronting whoever did this isn't something you can prepare for with a knife. Audrey didn't see it coming, and I don't want the same thing to happen to you. If you want to help her, instead of putting your own life in jeopardy, help me find the truth. We'll do it together, the right way."

Talia's jaw tightened, the light in her eyes shifting from defiance to something more guarded. For a moment, I thought she might argue my point, but then she sighed and pressed the button to close the knife.

She slipped it back into her pocket and turned toward me. "I know you're just trying to look out for me. It's just hard sitting around, doing nothing, while whoever did this to her gets to walk free."

"I know," I said. "But doing something reckless won't bring her back. She'd want you to stay alive, to honor her memory, and to live a full life, the life she never got to live."

We turned back toward the house, the forest going quiet as we made our exit.

"I'll be honest with you, because I think that's what you want from me," I said. "It won't feel normal for a while. Grief has a way of making every day feel the same, like you're stuck inside a moment that never ends. But one morning, you'll wake up and realize you made it through the night without crying. That's how it happens. Small steps. Little by little."

She nodded but said nothing.

"You'll never stop missing her," I said. "But the pain changes. It settles into something you can carry, something that reminds you of just how much she mattered."

The house came into view through the trees, which meant our time was coming to an end, and there was one more thing I hadn't talked to her about yet. As I glanced toward the kitchen window, Brianne's silhouette moved past, no doubt wondering where we'd been and what we'd talked about.

"There's something you should know, if you don't already," I said.

She looked at me, wary. "What is it?"

"It's about Logan. He's missing. He's been gone for five days now."

Talia blinked, confusion giving way to disbelief. "*Missing*? What do you mean, missing? Did he run off?"

"That's what it looks like," I said. "I was hoping you might know something that could point to where he went."

"I don't. He texted me a few times on the day Audrey died, and a couple of other times just to check in, but then he went quiet. I figured he needed space."

I pulled my phone from my pocket and scrolled to the photos I'd taken of the drawings from Logan's notebook and turned the phone toward her. "These are some of Logan's sketches. Do you recognize any of them?"

She studied the screen. "This one in the woods ... I don't know. He used to go camping or fishing on the weekends when he wanted to be alone. That was before he started dating Audrey. After, he never wanted to leave her side."

"What about this one?" I asked, showing her the sketch of the locket. "Have you ever seen it before?"

Talia frowned, taking a longer look. "I don't recognize it."

I flipped back a few photos, showing her the sketch of Audrey. "Do you know anything about this one?"

She nodded. "Yeah, he was making a portrait of Audrey as a graduation gift. He showed me the rough outline once. It's beautiful. Do you think, I mean, the night of the party when I saw them whispering ... do you think they knew something, that there was a secret they were keeping? You think that's why Logan's been gone for so long?"

"I don't know yet, but I hope to have some answers soon."

Talia crossed her arms. "If Logan's tied to Audrey's murder somehow, and if he's in danger, I hope you find him before whoever hurt Audrey finds him first."

10

Giovanni parked the car at the end of a narrow road that bled into the woods, and I glanced out my window, noticing the afternoon light filtering in through a canopy of pines. Beyond the trees, the faint outline of an old trail wound through the brush. It was part of the path I'd followed earlier with Talia.

"You sure this is the spot?" Giovanni asked, squinting toward the trees.

"I think so," I said, stepping out of the car. "If what Foley told me is right, the cabin should be somewhere around here."

We started walking, and after a while, I wasn't so sure Foley had given me the right directions, but then I saw the cabin sitting in a small clearing, its roof bowed inward at the center, the wood darkened with moss. One of its shutters was missing. The other was hanging on by a thread. The more I looked at it, the more the whole structure looked like it had exhaled and given up.

Giovanni turned toward me, giving a low whistle. "This place looks like it's about to collapse."

"I hope it doesn't, not until we get the chance to look around."

"I'd feel a whole lot better if you let me check it out first."

He phrased it as a statement rather than an option I was being given, so I held back as he stepped onto the porch, testing the boards before putting his weight down.

Turning toward me, he said, "It's sturdier than it looks."

I nodded and followed him inside, noting the air was cold and stale, carrying the scent of rot and something else I couldn't place. Light filtered in through a gap in the roof, spilling over a broken table and a scattering of debris on the floor.

"Someone's been here," I said, kneeling near the hearth. "See that?"

He leaned over my shoulder, and I pointed out the ashes in the fireplace. They were gray and compact, but the scent of smoke was long gone.

"It looks like it's been a while," he said.

"A few weeks, maybe a month, or even longer."

We searched the main room first. A few rusted nails clung to a wall where something had once hung, and in the far corner was a single wooden chair, which was missing a leg. I walked to it and flipped it over, checking out the seat. In the corner, the initials LL were carved into it inside a heart. I took a step back, studying the carving. The letters were somewhat fresh and deliberate, carved with a steady hand.

"This is interesting," I said.

Giovanni leaned in. "Do those initials mean anything to you?"

"Audrey was dating Logan Lambert. It makes sense that she carved it. And here's another one—AF."

"AF wouldn't be Audrey. Her last name is Ashford."

We kept looking.

I walked over to the remnants of what used to be a bed, curious to see if there was anything beneath it. "Hey, will you give me a hand?"

Giovanni nodded and joined me. We moved the bed to the side, and I noticed most of the floorboards beneath it were gone.

"Wonder what's down there," I said.

"Care to find out?"

I nodded, and he stepped out of the cabin, returning a minute later with a shovel. I gripped the handle, dragging it across the rotted floorboards as I made my way back over to the bed.

"Looks like some of the boards in this place have given out," he said.

"Or someone pulled them out and used the bed to cover it." I glanced around. "I don't see the missing floorboards anywhere, which seems strange to me. If they gave way, wouldn't they be here, in this hole?"

Beneath the splintered planks, it was hard to tell whether the dirt in the hole had ever been disturbed or not, but there was one way to find out.

I began to dig, a curious Giovanni looking on.

A few feet down, the dirt changed color, darker and wetter, perhaps seeping in from an abandoned body of water nearby. I knelt and began brushing it away with my hands, and then I saw something, a rock maybe. I wasn't sure. I dug around it with care until it came free.

"What have you found?" Giovanni asked.

"I don't know, but it's curved like the link of a chain. I don't think it's a rock."

I brushed the mud away with my fingers, though the grime clung tight, making it impossible to know what I'd found.

Perhaps nothing.

Perhaps something.

"I have a container of water in the car," I said. "Will you grab it for me?"

He stepped out a second time, unscrewing the lid off the bottle when he returned before handing it to me. I flattened the object in my hand and poured the water, using my thumb to help the grime break free. The water worked, and as I turned the object over in my palm, the shape was unmistakable.

"I think it's a bone," I said. "A human bone. A vertebrae from the looks of it."

Before I could inspect it further, a sound outside caught our attention, a crunch of leaves, quick and deliberate, indicating we weren't alone. Giovanni's gaze met mine, and on instinct, I shoved the bone fragment into my pocket, and we reached for our guns. We stepped out onto the porch. The woods beyond the clearing were still at first. Then came another sound, footsteps pounding through brush like someone was running.

Branches clawed at my jacket as I tore through the trees, following the rustle of movement until it vanished altogether.

I shouted, "Logan, stop," even though I did not know if he was the one we were chasing. By the time I reached the clearing, the person I was chasing was gone.

As Giovanni caught up to me, I lowered my weapon and scanned the tree line, trying to piece together who had been out here, what they were running from, and why.

"See anything?" he asked.

"Nothing. Whoever was out here was fast."

Giovanni holstered his gun, his eyes sweeping the trees one final time before we started back toward the cabin. The clearing felt different to me now, as if charged and uneasy.

When we reached the porch, I stopped short. In the dirt were fresh footprints. They were larger than mine and smaller than Giovanni's. Beside them, a single handprint was pressed deep into the soil near the car, as if someone had crouched there, waiting and watching.

Giovanni bent down to study it. "Whoever it was, they were close."

"Too close," I said.

11

By the time we reached the police department, the evidence bag holding the bone fragment was weighing on my mind. I couldn't help but wonder if there were more fragments back at the cabin, perhaps even an entire skeleton.

Giovanni parked out front, and we stepped inside. The place was buzzing with the usual noise. Phones ringing, conversations flowing, the copy machine humming.

Foley sat behind his desk, his glasses perched low on his nose as he read through a stack of reports. Whitlock leaned against the filing cabinet, arms folded, watching us with mild curiosity. I'd called on the drive over, letting them know we were coming and what we thought we'd found.

Foley didn't look up when we entered, instead saying, "Take a seat."

He continued perusing the papers in his hands for a moment, then slapped them down on the desk, giving me his full attention.

"Well, where's this discovery of yours?" he asked.

I reached into my handbag, pulling out the bone fragment and handing it to him.

He held it up to the light and frowned. "Where'd you find this again?"

"At the cabin. There's a hole beneath the bed where some floorboards used to be."

Foley raised a brow. "Hard to know if this is what we think it might be. If it is, it's hard to know how long it's been there and how it got there in the first place."

"I'm surprised the cabin wasn't searched better when your crew was there."

He looked at me as if I'd insulted him, and I realized I had.

"I wasn't trying to say you should have—"

He raised a hand. "Yes, you were. Don't bother backpedaling now. It's too late."

"If I offended you, I'm sorry."

"The cabin was searched, and yes, we could have been more thorough. But aside from the carved initials, we have no evidence linking it to Audrey's murder. It wasn't the crime scene. It's in the same woods, sure, but it's a different area with different terrain."

"When we were at the cabin, we poked around the place for a bit, but we didn't put much effort into it," Whitlock said. "Even so, this bone fragment is intriguing. I'll admit we could have done a better job searching the place."

Foley glared at Whitlock. "Thank you for stating the obvious. You're not helping, by the way."

"It's possible someone went to a lot of trouble to bury human remains beneath the old floorboards, thinking the cabin was abandoned and the remains would never be found," I said. "That's not nothing."

Whitlock pushed off the filing cabinet, studying the bone again. "How sure are we that it's a human bone?"

"We'll let the lab confirm," Foley said. "But it looks like part of a spine to me. Let's get Silas on the phone, see if he's free."

About thirty minutes later, Silas entered the office dressed in khaki pants, a long-sleeved button-up shirt with surfboards all over it, and clogs. He smoothed a hand down the side of his hair and smiled at me. "You rang?"

"Has anyone told you about the cabin in the woods not far from where Audrey was found?" I asked.

"They have."

"I found what I believe to be a piece of a human bone when I was there today."

Foley grabbed the evidence bag and handed it over, and Silas took a look.

"Is there any way for you to tell if it's human, and if so, how long it may have been in the ground?" I asked.

"Have you shown it to Simone? She used to be a forensic anthropologist, right?"

I nodded. "She's on vacation. I don't want to bother her."

"Well, let's see here ... We'll analyze it, focusing on its condition and chemical makeup. I'll want to see where you found it, so I can assess the soil conditions in the area."

"Is there anything you can tell me as far as initial observations?"

"Bones go through different decomposition stages. Fresh, crunchy, dry, smooth, ripple, and flake, to name a few. This helps establish time of death, but it's not exact. Did you find anything else around it?"

"We dug around for a while, but no, nothing. Do you think it's real, a human bone?"

"I do, but it doesn't mean I'm right. I won't know more until I run a few tests."

"The sooner, the better," Foley said. "In the meantime, we need to get back out to the cabin and see what else we can find."

12

I pulled into the lot behind the auto shop just as the first beams of morning light pushed over the ridge. The place was tucked between two warehouses, and as I walked to the garage, I noticed a patch of cracked pavement and scattered oil stains marking the ground like a badge of honor.

Inside, the garage door stood open, and the sound of metal tools echoed through the space, followed by a voice that rose above the clatter.

"Yo, give me a minute. I'll be right there."

A kid who was about college age emerged from behind a half-restored Camaro. He had a rag slung over one shoulder and a combination of dust and grease all over his arms. His thick blond hair fell across his forehead in uneven waves, and his gaze carried the sort of intensity that could draw one in or drive one back, depending on the situation.

He offered me a slight smile and said, "What can I do for you, ma'am?"

"Are you Colton Jagger?"

"I am."

"I'm Georgiana Germaine."

"Yeah, I've heard about you."

"From whom?"

He wiped his hands on the rag and leaned against the work-bench, studying me but not answering my question.

"I heard you've been making the rounds, though I'm not sure why you want to talk to me," he said.

"I'd like to ask you a few questions about Audrey."

His jaw tightened. "Figures."

I stepped around a discarded tire and got a little closer. "I'd like to know about how the two of you met, and what interactions you had with her."

"There's not much to tell. My first day at school, I saw her walking toward her locker, giggling with a couple of her friends. She flicked a piece of hair out of her face, looked back at me, and smiled. I thought she was the prettiest girl I'd ever seen. I asked a few of our classmates about her, and they told me she was dating Logan."

"You knew about Logan, and yet you still pursued her?"

"I mean, there are guys like Logan, and then there are guys like me. Didn't see him as much of a competition."

Guys like Logan.

What did *that* mean?

"You seem to have a high opinion of yourself," I said.

He swished a hand through the air. "Don't act like you don't know the feeling. I mean, look at you. If I was into cougars, you'd be at the top of my list."

"Let's keep the focus of this conversation on Audrey."

"Like I said before, there's not much to say. I made a move, she shut me down, and I backed off."

"That simple?"

"That simple," he said. "I don't chase women who aren't interested."

"How long after you showed interest in Audrey did you begin spending time with Talia?"

His eyes flickered, suggesting he was uncomfortable with the question.

"Talia's super chill and easy to be around. So yeah, we started hanging out right after Audrey said she wasn't interested."

"Were you spending time with Talia to make Audrey jealous, or because you were hoping to spend more time with Audrey, or ..."

He pushed off the workbench. "It was nothing like that. Audrey missed school because she was sick one day, and Talia passed me in the hall and asked if I wanted to grab lunch. I figured, why not? We started hanging out here and there, and the more we got to know each other, the more we realized we had a lot in common."

I may not have known Talia long, but from the brief interaction we'd had, they seemed like opposites.

"Audrey didn't like that you and Talia spent time together," I said. "Were you aware of that?"

He hesitated. "Talia mentioned it to me a couple of times. It didn't change anything for me. It was something they needed to figure out."

"That's it?"

"I don't know what more you want me to say. I didn't see why Audrey was so bent over us hanging out. If she wasn't interested in me, why should it have mattered?"

He was confident.

Almost *too* confident.

"Where were you the night Audrey died?" I asked.

"I'll tell you what I told the police. As far as a timeline, I don't remember every detail of that night."

"What *do* you remember?"

He rubbed a hand across his brow. "I think I was at the arcade. I spend a lot of nights there when I get off work. It's a good place to keep my mind off stuff."

"What stuff?"

"I don't know. Stuff."

His vagueness was getting on my nerves.

"Were you alone?" I asked.

"At the arcade? Lots of people hang out there."

"What I mean to say is—were you there with anyone you know, anyone who can give you an alibi?"

"Lots of people were there, but none of them were friends of mine."

I was getting nowhere, the conversation looping around in circles, which he didn't seem to mind. Time to shift gears.

"Tell me about your home life, your parents, and your siblings, if you have any," I said.

"Why?"

"Why not?" I said, looking him in the eye.

He met my gaze head on with a guarded calm that made my instincts sharpen.

"I have one brother," he said. "He's older than I am."

"How much older?"

"A few years. Left home when he was sixteen."

"Where is he now?"

"I don't know. Haven't heard from him in, oh ... about nine months, I guess."

I crossed my arms. "I feel like there's a story there."

"There isn't."

"And your parents? What are they like?"

"My mom works two jobs, sometimes three. Don't see her much."

"And your dad?"

"He doesn't work."

"What's your relationship with him like?"

He turned, staring at a dented toolbox near the car he'd been working on. "We don't have one."

"Why not?"

"He's a drunk, for starters."

I thought back to the comment he'd made about the arcade being a good place to keep his mind off stuff—*stuff* tied to his father among other things, I guessed.

"Look, I don't mind talking to you, but not about my family," he said.

"All right, fine. Going back to the night Audrey died, did you see her that day?"

"I didn't, and just so we're clear, I never laid a hand on Audrey, and I didn't follow her into the forest that night. I wouldn't have ever done anything to hurt her, or any other woman for that matter. I get that you're looking for a suspect, but you can chase down every shadow in this town. You won't trace one back to me."

His comment struck me as odd.

"When I mentioned Talia, you gave me a look that leads me to believe she's more than a friend. Is she?"

"Ask her."

"I will, later. Right now, I'm asking you."

"Fine," he said. "We're dating."

"For how long?"

"Since a few weeks before Audrey died."

"Why keep it a secret?"

"Talia knew Audrey wouldn't approve."

"Audrey's opinion no longer matters, so why keep the truth from everyone now?"

He shrugged. "We haven't talked about it since Audrey died. Talia's been having a hard time, so it doesn't feel like the right moment to put our relationship on blast, not when there's a sick psycho murderer out there."

A sick psycho murderer.

I liked the label.

"Do Talia's parents know about your relationship?" I asked.

"They didn't before, but now that Talia's spending most of her time in her room, I've gone to her house a lot more than usual. They haven't said anything to me, but I think they suspect something's going on."

"What about your friends? Do they know?"

He shook his head. "A few. I felt kinda guilty."

"About what?"

"Talia told me Audrey hated secrets, and she hated lies even more. They fought about it once. Big fight. I walked in on it. Audrey called me trouble, and Talia said she didn't know me well enough to judge me the way she did."

"Do you agree with Talia's assessment of you?"

He ran a hand through his hair. "Yeah, but hey, sometimes I think I don't even know myself. You know what I mean?"

"I do. There have been times in my life when I've questioned everything about myself."

"*You?* I can't believe it. You look like the most well-put-together person I've ever met."

"I suppose I am —*now*. It wasn't always that way. Going back to the argument between Talia and Audrey ... is there anything else I should know?"

He gave the question some thought. "Maybe one thing. Talia accused Audrey of keeping a secret herself."

"How did Audrey react?"

"She stormed out of the room and left."

"Do you think Audrey was keeping a secret?"

"I don't know. I guess it's possible she saw something she

shouldn't have or knew something she shouldn't have, and someone murdered her because of it."

A man exited an office, narrowing his eyes at Colton as he said, "What did you do with the wrench?"

"Check the desk. I may have left it there when I went to answer the phone." The man nodded, and Colton turned toward me. "I need to get back to work."

"One more question. When was the last time you saw Audrey?"

He blinked, going quiet, and for a moment the two of us stood there in silence.

"What aren't you telling me?" I asked.

"It's nothing."

"It's something."

"It's not that I don't want to tell you. I do. I just don't want to get myself in trouble."

"What kind of trouble?"

"Trouble with the law."

"I'm not the law. I'm a private investigator."

"Doesn't mean you won't snitch."

"Unless it's something major, like you confessing to Audrey's murder or having any part in it, your secret's safe with me."

He glanced outside at a man who had just pulled up in a shiny blue truck.

"My boss is here," he said.

"Then we better make this quick."

He took a deep breath in and said, "I'm older than I look. I've had to repeat a couple of school years more than once."

It was a confession, but I wasn't sure what he was getting at.

"And?" I asked.

"I'm twenty-one. If I get caught at parties with my classmates from school, I'd be seen as contributing to the delinquency of minors."

"Is this your way of saying you were at one of those parties and you witnessed something?"

"Not witnessed. Overheard."

I leaned in closer. "I'm listening."

"I was coming around the corner, and I saw Audrey huddled in the corner with Logan. They didn't see me when I walked by, but when I did, she said something to him about worrying she wasn't safe. Then she said if *she* wasn't safe, *he* wasn't safe either."

Hearing his words, it felt like everything had just tightened around me.

If Audrey was right, and someone ended her life to keep their secret from being exposed, I now understood why Logan had vanished.

13

Sadie Holt lived in a stucco house on a quiet cul-de-sac lined with identical mailboxes and trimmed hedges. When I pulled to a stop in front of the house, the garage door was open, and a little pink sedan was parked inside. I hoped the car was Sadie's and that the lack of other vehicles meant the seventeen-year-old was home alone and that I had her all to myself.

I parked in the driveway, got out of the car, and walked to the door, ringing the bell. A shuffle of feet sounded inside, followed by the click of a lock. The door cracked open an inch, and one pale-blue eye blinked out at me.

"If you're looking for my parents, they aren't home," she said.

"Are you Sadie?"

"Yeah."

"I'm not here to talk to your parents. I'm here to talk to you."

"Why?"

She pulled the door open all the way and leaned against the frame. Her long blond hair hung in two loose braids over her shoulders, and she wore sweats and an oversized sweater that swallowed her tiny frame. As we stood there, staring at each other, her expression shifted a few times, going from curiosity to irritation to boredom.

"I'm Georgiana Germaine," I said.

"I don't care who you are."

"Rosemary Ashford hired me to investigate her daughter's murder."

"Ahh, you're the private investigator," she said. "The one everyone in town has been talking about."

"I am, and I'd like to ask you a few questions about Audrey."

She groaned as if I'd asked her to scrub the floor with a toothbrush. "Why? I'm not involved with what happened to her, and besides, I don't feel like answering your questions."

"If you don't want to talk to me now, fine. But you should know I'll keep coming around until you do."

She rolled her eyes as if she found me annoying.

"Fiiiiine, come in," she said. "But I have somewhere to be in an hour, so make it quick."

She stepped aside, and I entered a living room filled with mismatched furniture, a wall of crystal animals in various shapes and sizes, and a faint cinnamon smell in the air.

Sadie flopped onto a beanbag and curled her legs beneath her.

"You can sit or whatever," she said.

I sat across from her. "If it would make you feel more comfortable, you can let your parents know I'm here."

"They don't need to know," she said with a shrug. "Why are you here?"

"I'd like to know about your friendship with Audrey."

Her jaw tightened. "We used to be close. Then we weren't. That's the story. Are we done?"

"Not yet. I'm going to need a little more than that."

Sadie let out a frustrated sigh. "Fine. We were friends. Then she stole from me. End of story."

"You're referring to the night of the party."

"Yeah, the one where everyone assumed I'd had too much to drink and forced me to leave the party while they all stayed. Real fun night."

"You left your purse behind."

Sadie crossed her arms and leaned back, grabbing a blanket that was puddled on the floor and threw it over her legs. "If you know the story already, why are we talking about it?"

"I'd like to hear it from your perspective."

She huffed a frustrated sigh. "I left my purse, Audrey found it, and she took it home. When I picked it up the next morning, 200 bucks was missing. That was my allowance for the whole week."

One week?

Spoiled much?

"Audrey told you she didn't take the money, didn't she?" I asked.

"I mean, yeah, but come on. Who else would have done it?"

"Anyone else at the party. Did you have proof that she took it?"

"I didn't need proof." Her voice rose, brittle and defensive, then softened just as fast. "The next week, she showed up at school with a new backpack, one she'd been eyeing for a while. I asked her where she got the money for it, and she said she'd opened a store online and was selling some bracelets she'd made. I wasn't buying it."

"*Had* she opened a store?"

Sadie shrugged. "I dunno. All I know is, we weren't the same after that. She was offended when I accused her, and she said she couldn't trust me anymore. Funny thing. Trust goes both ways."

"Did you ever consider the possibility that someone else took the money?"

She glared at me. "You sound like Talia."

"In what way?"

"She wanted me to believe Audrey didn't care about money. Please. Everyone cares about money."

Her tone swung again, confident at first, then becoming a little more vulnerable.

"What happened when you accused Audrey of taking the money?" I asked.

"She cried. Like big, dramatic tears. She was hurt that I'd called her a thief."

"Did the two of you ever resolve things before she died?"

"No." She paused. "And now I kinda wish we had. I've thought about the day we argued about the money, and you know, even if she took it, I'll admit she'd always been a good friend to me before that, and I'd allowed it all to be thrown away over a bit of cash."

The confession surprised me almost as much as it seemed to surprise her.

She glanced away, fingers picking at a loose thread on her sweater.

"When was the last time you saw Audrey?" I asked.

"A few days before she died at a fast-food joint in town. She looked stressed, and she kept checking her phone, but I don't know why. We saw each other, but we didn't talk. It's weird, you know. Her dying in the one place she loved most."

"In the woods, you mean?"

"Yeah. She grew up playing in those woods. She told me that was the place she went to feel calm. What she found there the night she died was anything but that."

Her voice wavered, then she cleared her throat.

"Even though you two weren't speaking much before she

died, I hope you try to remember all the good times you had," I said.

"I do. You ... ahh, you're not here because you think I killed her, right?"

"I'm just here to ask questions and to see where the answers lead. And to get to the truth, to the heart of what happened to her and why."

"You sound like my therapist," she muttered.

"You have a therapist?"

"Don't know why you're so shocked. Half the kids in our school need one. Maybe even a little more than half."

I switched topics. "Where were you on the day Audrey died?"

"At home."

"Were your parents around?"

"No, they were out."

First Colton and his vague recollection about being at the arcade on the day Audrey died, and now it seemed Sadie didn't have an alibi either.

"Did you ever see Audrey arguing with anyone at school, or did she have any issues with any of her classmates, aside from what happened with you, I mean?"

"Audrey was a gentle soul, the kind of person who might tear up if you looked at her the wrong way. She preferred peace over confrontation."

"What can you tell me about her relationship with Logan?"

"They were two peas in a pod, soulmates who were meant to be together. He'd had a crush on her ever since they were kids. We all knew it."

"Logan has been missing for several days. Did you know that?"

She raised a brow, her expression one of concern. "I didn't. Aww, man, I can't imagine what he's going through. It's so sad.

He'd finally worked up the nerve to tell her how he felt, and then, she ... you know ..."

Had the life snuffed out of her.

"Any idea where I could find him?" I asked.

"We're friends, but not that good of friends. I'd ask Willow Robinson. She knows him a lot better."

Willow and McKenna were the other two classmates who'd planned to go on the weekend trip with Talia and Audrey—a trip cut short by Audrey's murder. I planned to speak with them both.

"I've just been to see Colton Jagger," I said. "He admitted he's dating Talia. Did you know?"

"She's never come right out and said it, but I suspected as much. Before Audrey died, I saw them together a lot."

"I'm sure it must have been awkward for Audrey. I heard she wasn't too happy about them hanging out."

Sadie wiggled around, adjusting herself in the beanbag chair. "After I accused Audrey of stealing the money from my bag, we didn't talk much, so I have no idea what she thought about Colton and Talia. I think he's weird."

"Colton?"

She nodded.

"In what way?" I asked.

"He always seems to show up everywhere. I go to the store, he's there. Stop at the gas station, he's there. It's creepy. Gives me stalker vibes."

"We live in a small town. I see the same people all the time. It doesn't mean they're stalking me."

"Small towns are that way. Everyone getting all up in everyone else's business."

She had a point.

"Was Colton ever aggressive toward Audrey?" I asked.

"Not that I saw. But he stared at her a lot. When he first moved here, he made a point to let everyone know he liked her."

"He told me Audrey made it clear she wasn't interested. He backed off after that."

She shrugged. "Who knows? Maybe he did. I don't know. I just thought it was weird that when he failed to get Audrey, he started talking to Talia. It's so cringe."

I didn't speak fluent teen, but every once in a while, I managed to understand their lingo. *Cringe* was their word for something that made a person feel embarrassed, uncomfortable, or awkward.

"Do you know anyone who would have wanted to harm Audrey?" I asked.

She tapped her fingers on her knee, thinking.

"I know I didn't treat her the way I should have right before she died, but I can say she was one of the most caring friends I've ever had."

"I'm hearing that a lot."

"That's why none of this makes any sense. I can't think of any reason why someone would kill her."

I took a moment to decide how much I wanted to say. "Did you have a classmate named Anne?"

"*Anne*? No, I don't think so. Why?"

Admitting what I'd seen in Logan's notebook would mean admitting I'd gone into his room without permission. I decided it was best to keep that to myself unless I knew I could trust the person.

"Did you ever see Logan or Audrey with a locket?"

I described it to her.

"I don't think so," she said. "You're asking a lot of weird questions."

"I get how you see it that way. Let's just say there are some details I can share about the case and others I can't."

She leaned forward, resting her hands on her knees. "After all I've told you, I feel like I deserve something. Come on. One little detail won't hurt. You may not have solved her murder yet, but I bet you have some idea why she was killed. Am I right?"

I crossed my arms. "I haven't been able to prove it yet, but I believe Audrey stumbled upon something she shouldn't have, and she was killed to keep her quiet."

Her gaze locked with mine, sharp and bright. "And Logan? Do you think he's involved?"

"I'm leaning toward yes."

"Man, that sucks. Hope he comes home."

I stood. "Well, I think I've covered everything I can think to ask for now."

She grabbed her cell phone and boosted herself off the beanbag chair. I followed her to the door. She opened it, turning back to say, "This is just my opinion, but I don't think the person you're looking for is anyone from our school."

"Why's that?"

"I dunno, just a vibe I'm getting."

I stepped onto the porch, the door closing behind me with a soft click. As I walked to the car, her last words circled in my mind. She was certain none of their classmates had killed Audrey. If she was right, then someone outside that tight group had slipped into Audrey's life, unseen and unchecked, hiding in a place I hadn't thought to look yet.

14

I pulled into the driveway at home just as the last bit of the evening's light faded behind the pines. The sky over Cambria was gorgeous tonight, sweeping bands of orange, pink, and deep gold across the horizon. I stepped out of the car and saw a beaming Luka, ears perked up, happy I was home.

I stepped inside the house and was met with the aroma of garlic and tomatoes drifting from the kitchen. Giovanni whistled, and Luka barreled past, skidding across the kitchen tile and bumped his head against Giovanni's leg. Giovanni bent down, giving him a quick scratch behind the ear before going back to stirring a pot of sauce on the stove.

He glanced over at me and smiled. "How was your day?"

"Long, but productive."

I set my bag on the table and slipped off my coat, a vintage wool A-line with faux fur trim.

Tonight, Giovanni was dressed in fitted charcoal slacks and a pressed black button-up beneath an apron. His dark hair was slicked back, and not a single strand was out of place, as usual. He looked tired, but his eyes were warm as they took me in.

Turning his attention to the sauce, he lifted out a spoonful, blew on it, and gave it a taste test. He then nodded in satisfaction and turned off the burner, saying, "Sit, and tell me everything that's happened since we were at the cabin earlier today."

I sank into a chair at the table, and Luka settled at my feet with a soft huff. Giovanni set two bowls on the table, filled them with pasta and sauce, and then he took a seat across from me.

"At the cabin, we were still piecing together what we knew," I said. "Things like Audrey being murdered in those woods, Logan going missing, and the mysterious locket in his sketchbook. After the day I've had, all those discoveries feel like a lifetime ago. Since then, I've met with Colton and Sadie, two of Audrey's classmates."

"Why them?"

"Colton hasn't lived here long. When he first started at the school, Audrey caught his attention. He found out she was in a relationship, but it didn't stop him from pursuing her."

Giovanni raised a brow, his tone turning dry. "Sounds like a stand-up guy."

"He's full of himself, that much is clear. He told me Audrey turned him down, and not long after, he started hanging out with Talia, her best friend. Audrey wasn't happy about it, but they kept seeing each other, and today I found out they're dating, but they've been keeping it quiet."

"Did he say why?"

"He doesn't feel like it's the right time to make it public, given Audrey was just murdered. He also told me he was at a party, and he overheard Audrey telling Logan she didn't feel safe, and that she was worried he wasn't either."

Giovanni's expression turned serious. "Now she's dead, and Logan is nowhere to be found. It seems Audrey may have predicted what was to come."

I nodded. "I keep thinking back to Logan's drawing of the

locket with the name *Anne* on it. I just wish I knew its relevance, and if it's related to the case somehow."

"I have no doubt you'll figure it out. You always do. How was your visit with Sadie?"

"Sadie and Audrey had a falling out over 200 hundred dollars that went missing from Sadie's purse after she left it at a party. Audrey had found the purse and took it home with her. When Sadie picked it up the next day, she noticed the cash was gone. Audrey denied taking the money, and whether she took it or not, the accusation damaged their relationship."

"Why did Sadie make such an accusation? I imagine there were plenty of other people at that party who could have taken it."

"I had the same argument. Sadie said Audrey bought a new backpack right after she got her purse back. When Sadie asked her about it, Audrey claimed she paid for the backpack with money she received from an online store she'd started."

Giovanni ate while he listened, his focus steady.

"Sadie also said she saw Audrey at a fast-food place a few days before the murder," I said. "They didn't speak, but she noticed Audrey watching her phone, looking tense."

"And does Sadie have an alibi during the time of the murder?" he asked.

"A thin one at best. She said she was at home, but she was alone, so no one can confirm whether she's telling the truth or not. Colton's alibi isn't solid either. He *thinks* he was at the arcade that night."

Giovanni finished his pasta, pushed the bowl to the side, and crossed his arms.

"Where does that leave you in your investigation?" he asked.

"It leaves me with more questions than answers."

"Which question would you like to be answered first?"

"I want to know who Anne is, and if she is or was a real person. I asked Sadie if they had a classmate named Anne, and she didn't think they did."

"Maybe Anne's not a classmate," Giovanni said. "Maybe he drew the sketch with the intention of giving it to someone, a relative perhaps."

"Or maybe it isn't a relative, and she's tied to the case somehow."

I took a few more bites of pasta, grabbed my bowl and his, and carried them to the sink, rinsing them while Giovanni moved to the small desk tucked beside the kitchen window. His laptop waited there, still open from the project he was working on, a hotel his family was renovating in New York City.

I dried my hands and joined him, pulling up a chair.

"I'm not even close to as good as you are with your sleuthing, but we don't have anything else to do tonight," he said. "What do you say we do a little searching and see what we can find?"

"I think it's a great idea."

Giovanni tapped a finger on of the keys, and the screen lit up, its soft glow washing over his face.

"All right," he said. "What do we search first?"

"Start simple," I said. "Try typing in the words 'Anne Cambria woods.'"

He typed in what I'd said, hit enter, and a list of search results filled the screen.

"Not much information here," he said. "We have an Anne who runs a gift shop, an Anne who writes poems about tide pools, and an article about a woman named Ann without an E who leads some of the birdwatching tours in town."

"Nothing stands out about any of them," I said. "Try searching 'Anne locket California.'"

He cleared the search bar and typed again.

"Still nothing," he said.

I stared at the screen, my frustration building.

Given the bone fragment we'd found, I wondered if there was more to Anne, and my thoughts turned to more sinister events.

"Maybe we need to cast a wider net," I suggested. "Let's say Anne does exist. She may not live in Cambria."

"Good point."

"Try 'unsolved cases San Luis Obispo County' and add a time frame, let's say in the past thirty years."

He typed in what I'd suggested, added dates, and the results were different this time. As we read down the page, I pointed to one entry in particular. "There, click on that one, 'local teen still missing after twenty-five years.'"

Giovanni clicked on the link.

The article opened with a grainy photo of a girl with shoulder-length dark hair and a wide, hopeful smile. Her name was Anne Fontaine. Anne had grown up in Morro Bay, and at the age of seventeen she'd vanished while spending the summer with her aunt in Cambria.

No body, no witnesses, and no arrests.

But now I was certain Anne Fontaine and the locket Logan sketched were connected to Audrey somehow.

As I read further, the article went on to explain that Anne's aunt, Glinda Potts, lived in the Harvest Creek subdivision at the time, a fact that made my skin prickle.

"Anne stayed with her aunt the summer she went missing," I said. "And her aunt just so happened to live in the same subdivision Audrey's parents live in now. It's a big coincidence, isn't it? What are the odds Audrey and Anne both hiked in the same forest?"

"I'd say the odds are high."

I stood, pacing the room, thinking.

A few minutes later, a theory came to light.

"I believe Audrey visited the cabin at least once, but I'd guess it was more often than that. When she was there, she carved Logan's initials into the wood. She also tidied up, maybe thinking she'd turned the old cabin into her own private sanctuary. While cleaning, she found a locket inscribed with Anne's name, and I bet she also found the initials AF carved into the wood."

"Seems plausible to me."

"What if, while Audrey was cleaning, she started digging around in the hole beneath the bed and she discovered what we did—a bone, or multiple bones even. She tells Logan about the bone and the locket, which is why he sketched it. Maybe the two of them started doing some investigating, and they figured out the locket belonged to Anne Fontaine, the girl who went missing."

"If you're right, and I'd say you are, I understand why Logan left when he did."

"I need to locate him. The sooner the better. But first, let's see if we can find information on Anne's aunt and her parents, and see if they still live in the county."

Giovanni nodded, turning back to the computer and entered a new search for Violet and Eugene Fontaine. Another article popped up, one written by a local reporter on the twentieth anniversary of Anne's disappearance. The reporter had interviewed Violet outside the small house where she and Eugene still lived. The caption under the photo named the street.

"I wonder if they still live in the same house," I said.

Giovanni clicked on the article. It repeated some of the facts we'd already read and then described a small display of photos and candles that Violet kept near the front window. In one candlelit picture, I spotted a faint glint near Anne's throat.

"Can you zoom in on this photo of Anne?" I asked.

He nodded. The bigger the photo got, the more blurred it was, but even so, it held enough detail for us to see what appeared to be a silver locket hanging from a chain around Anne's neck.

"That seals it for me," I said. "Audrey and Logan knew about the locket, and they must have tied it to the cold case."

"It would explain why Audrey was worried that they weren't safe. Someone must have found out she had the locket."

I sat back down, and Luka sauntered over, laying his head on my lap. "It's been twenty-five years. I'd say Anne isn't just missing; I'd say she's dead, and no one has found her body yet."

"I need to speak to Whitlock, and to Foley," I said. "But Foley's out with my sister tonight. It's their anniversary. I'll start with Whitlock and get him to dig up everything they have on the cold case."

Giovanni gave a small nod. "He will love that."

"He will," I said. "Solving two cases instead of one, and a cold case to boot. I must admit, the idea is exciting."

I reached for my phone and made the call. Whitlock picked up on the second ring.

"Georgiana," he said. "Is everything all right?"

"I have a theory."

"I've been waiting for you to say as much. What is it?"

"Twenty-five years ago, a girl named Anne Fontaine was visiting Cambria over the summer, and she went missing," I said.

"I remember. I was one of the detectives who worked on the case. What does Anne have to do with the reason you called?"

"I think her locket turned up in our woods, and I think Audrey found it. Now Audrey is dead and Logan is missing. If you're not too busy, head over, and I'll explain everything to you in person."

He went quiet for a moment and then said, "I'll swing by the station, grab the old files if I can find them, and be right over."

15

Morning light washed over the hills as Whitlock and I drove along the coastal highway. Waves rolled against the shoreline below, a slow rhythm that fed into the theories running through my mind. We'd stayed up late the night before, going over Anne's cold case. In the end, we felt we were both heading in a direction that would lead us to Audrey's killer.

Beside me, Whitlock drummed his fingers on the steering wheel. "So, we had a lot to talk about last night, didn't we? Chasing clues is like piecing together a shattered mirror, each shard reflecting a sliver of the bigger picture. Wouldn't you agree?"

"Nice metaphor, and yes, I agree."

He smoothed a hand over his floral tie, adjusting it. "It was interesting, going through the evidence box from Anne's cold case. I remember the scarf was found not too far from her aunt's house. Anne's mother swore the scarf belonged to her daughter. She even showed me a photo of her wearing it to prove her point."

"Back then, DNA wasn't what it is now."

"It sure wasn't, which is why I dropped the scarf off to Silas this morning. DNA, hair and fibers, body fluids, skin oils, gunshot residue ... old threads hold on to them longer than people expect sometimes."

"It reminds me of Catherine Eddowes, Jack the Ripper's fourth victim. It's been over 130 years since her death, and yet reexamined DNA evidence of the semen on her shawl matched the descendants of Polish barber Aaron Kosminski, one of the suspects back then. What do you think of that?"

Whitlock shrugged. "I don't know what to make of it. What about you?"

"I'm not sure either. Among scientists, it seems to be up for debate."

"Yeah, well, I'm hopeful Silas finds something we didn't have the ability to find before."

"Me too."

Morro Bay came into view, the harbor sitting calm, boats bobbing in the soft shine of morning. A gull swooped low and cruised alongside us for a few seconds before changing paths and veering toward the water.

Though Anne and Audrey's stories had been separated by decades, I got the feeling they shared a similar spine, perhaps a shared secret even.

We turned onto a quiet residential street, and Whitlock slowed down as he scanned the house numbers. The Fontaine home sat near the end of the block. It was a small one-story wood home with blue shutters and a garden that looked like it hadn't been tended to for some time.

Whitlock parked in the driveway and turned toward me. "Before we go inside, I'll tell you what I remember about Anne's parents. I recall Violet being a sweet, kindhearted woman, easy to talk to, and the kind of person who wears her heart on her sleeve."

"Good to know. And Eugene?"

"Eugene is … well, much different. He sometimes answers questions or responds to things without a lot of tact. That's the way I remember him, anyway. He could have changed, I suppose, but I imagine he hasn't. Oh, and one more thing," he said, lifting a finger. "Eugene is Anne's stepfather."

"Who's her biological father?"

"A man who died when Anne was a child, though I don't remember the specifics."

We walked up the path toward the house, and Whitlock knocked on the door. A moment later, it opened.

A stout woman with soft silver hair that was curled at the ends blinked at us and smiled. She wore a pale pink cardigan over a white T-shirt and jeans, and as the morning chill kicked up, she pulled the cardigan tighter around her waist.

"Goodness gracious, it's been too long," she said to Whitlock, moving a hand to her hip. "You haven't changed one bit. It's as if you're aging in reverse."

Whitlock smiled. "I was just about to say the same thing to you."

She laughed and pressed a hand to her chest. "Come in. Please. Both of you."

We followed her into the house, a cozy little place that smelled of newspapers and old books. In the living room, a wall dedicated to Anne was filled with photos of her from birth all the way up to when she went missing.

It wasn't long before Eugene entered from the kitchen. He was tall and thin and had a weathered face that suggested he'd been through a lot in life. He wore a loose white shirt with red suspenders that did a poor job of holding up his pants.

"What brings you two here?" he asked.

His tone, while not hostile, was one of worry.

Whitlock clasped his hands together. "Eugene, it's a pleasure to see you after so much time has passed. Allow me to introduce Georgiana Germaine, a private investigator working with the department on one of our cases."

"You reopen Anne's case or something? Is that why you're here?"

"In a way. That's what we want to talk to you about."

Eugene crossed his arms. "I'll tell you now what I told you then. Anne didn't run away, as one of the other detectives you worked with back then suggested. Someone took her, and we've made peace with the fact that she's not coming back."

Violet reached for Eugene's arm. "We don't even know what they're here to talk to us about yet, honey. We should hear them out first, don't you think?"

Eugene nodded. "Let's all take a seat. I've just brewed up a pot of coffee, if anyone is interested."

We passed on the coffee and sat down.

"We're here because we're working on a case that may be linked to Anne's disappearance," I said.

Violet gasped, raising a hand to her mouth. "After all this time? Has another young woman gone missing?"

"Not missing," Whitlock said. "She was murdered."

Eugene and Violet exchanged concerned glances.

"Then how ..." Violet started. "How could they be connected? I don't understand."

Whitlock leaned toward her, his voice gentle. "We believe the young woman who was murdered spent some time at a cabin just outside of the Harvest Creek subdivision. We've found some interesting things there."

"Like what?" Eugene asked.

Whitlock tipped his head toward me, as if suggesting I do the honors.

"The young woman's name is Audrey Ashford. She was walking through the woods not far from the cabin on the night she was murdered. I searched the cabin and found what I believe to have been your daughter's initials carved into a wood beam."

"Tell her about the locket," Whitlock said.

"When Audrey died, she was dating a boy named Logan. In one of his sketchbooks, I found a drawing of a locket. It was silver and oval in shape. Along the outer edge was a delicate ring of hearts, and in the center was Anne's name."

Violet's eyes filled with tears. "She never took that locket off. Not once. It was a gift from her aunt. Will you excuse me for a moment?"

We nodded, and Violet pushed her chair back and left the room.

She returned with a framed photo, which she handed to me. "Is this the locket the young man drew?"

I stared at the picture for some time, even though I recognized the locket in an instant.

"It is the one he drew, yes."

"But how ... after all this time?"

"I have a theory, which I haven't proven yet. My gut tells me Anne and Audrey had both been to the cabin before, even though it was decades apart. I was there yesterday, and it looked like someone had tried to tidy it up in recent months. I think Audrey found the locket inside the cabin, and she got curious and decided to try and find out who Anne was and what happened to her."

"Georgiana's theories are almost always right," Whitlock said.

Violet lowered herself into a chair and drifted into silence, the air seeming to tighten around us as we waited to hear what she'd say next. When she spoke again, the words landed like a sharp blow. "I believe your theory about Anne visiting the cabin, and I know who built it."

16

"The cabin was built by my grandfather," Violet said. "He inherited the land from his father, and back then, part of it looked much like it still does today, I imagine. My grandfather loved those woods, and when he was a teenager, he built that cabin as a place to go when he wanted to be alone with his thoughts."

Whitlock shook his head, staring at Violet in shock. "Why didn't you tell me this when your daughter went missing?"

"I didn't think it was relevant. The last time Anne was seen was at the Boathouse Diner in town, which, as you both know, is miles away from the cabin. At the time, I didn't know about Anne's interest in the cabin or that she'd been to it."

"I feel like I'm missing a good deal of this story," I said.

"I apologize," Violet said. "Let me start from the beginning. When my grandfather was in his sixties, a developer approached him about buying the land to build a subdivision."

"Are you talking about Harvest Creek?"

Violet nodded. "Those woods were just as much a part of him as the breath he drew. Still, he needed money. So, my grandfather agreed to sell part of the land to the developer and to preserve the other part for future generations, with a clause in his will that it would never be sold."

"You said you didn't know your daughter had any interest in the cabin, but when we were talking before you said you believed Anne had been there," I said.

Violet crossed one leg over the other. "A few years ago, my sister Glinda came for a visit, and we got to talking about Anne and the last summer they spent together. That is when I learned about Anne's fascination with our family history, and Glinda told her about the cabin, and why our grandfather built it."

"Why hadn't Anne ever heard about the cabin before?"

"I was three years old when my grandfather died, and I have no memory of him. Glinda was much older and much more sentimental in nature. After she told Anne about the cabin, she warned her not to go inside, since it's no longer, what you would call, 'structurally sound.'"

"But you believe she went there anyway."

"Anne was curious in nature. When you showed up here today, talking about the cabin and the locket Audrey may have found, I was in shock. I never would have considered the cabin a place to look for clues. How naïve I've been all these years."

"I wouldn't say you're naïve," Whitlock said. "You only became aware a few years ago that Anne knew of its existence."

Eugene, who'd been quiet for some time, stood and refreshed his coffee. Then he returned to the table.

Whitlock cleared his throat. "I know we went over this a while ago, and I don't know about you, but when I looked over all my notes, I have to say, some of them were confusing. Guess what I'm saying is, we'd like to hear anything you can share about the summer Anne went missing. Any detail. No matter how small it seems."

Violet shifted in her chair, thinking. "Anne stayed with my

sister Glinda that summer, as you know. They both shared a love for Cambria I never seemed to understand, and Glinda cherished the times they had together. She told me they often walked through the forest, hiked the trails, and explored as much of the outdoors as they could."

"Did Anne ever mention anyone she hung around with during those summer visits?" I asked.

"Oh, I don't know. I never heard about any friends she may have made."

"Tell her about the man," Eugene said.

"Oh, yes. One day when Glinda and Anne were out walking in the neighborhood, they passed by a man walking in the opposite direction. They waved, and he did the same. Glinda didn't recognize him, and she thought he was new in town."

Eugene cut in. "Glinda said they were coming out of their house one morning, and he was across the street, staring at her house," Eugene said. "She thought something was off about him."

Whitlock leaned forward. "It's all coming back to me now. I remember talking to you about him."

"Your partner brushed it off," Eugene said.

"He may have, but I didn't. The guy had a tattoo of a cross on his ankle, didn't he?"

Violet nodded, and I thought about a man in town who had a tattoo just like the one she'd described.

"Does your sister still live in the same house?" I asked.

"No, she passed away a couple of years ago."

"I'm sorry to hear it," I said.

"It's all right. She lived a long and happy life. She's in a better place now."

"Do you remember anything else unusual around that time?" Whitlock asked.

"Not about that time, but a few months after Anne went

missing, Eugene and I went to Cambria. We stayed with my sister. One morning, I went out to get the paper, and a man was parked in a truck a couple of houses down, just staring at me. I thought he might have been the same man Anne and Glinda saw on their walk."

Eugene stiffened. "Hun, we don't know that he was the same man. You didn't get a good look at him."

"He was a mysterious man sitting in a dark truck for who knows what reason," Violet said. "I told Glinda about him, and she thought it was suspicious too."

"Did the man see you looking at him?" I asked.

"Yes," she whispered. "He stared at me for a minute and then started his truck and drove off."

Whitlock let out a slow breath. "This is the first I'm hearing about it."

"You were out of town when it happened," Eugene said. "We talked to your partner. We assumed he told you."

"Yeah, well, he should have, but he didn't."

"Do you remember anything about the man?" I asked. "Do you know his hair color, what he was wearing, or his build?"

Violet yawned, looking at Eugene. "I think I'll take that cup of coffee now."

He nodded and rose to get it for her.

Turning toward me, she said, "He was wearing a baseball cap the day I saw him, and he had a beard. It was rough, like he didn't shave often. Glinda told me the man she saw also had a beard."

"How old did he look?"

"Around the same age I was at the time."

Whitlock removed a pen from his pocket and scribbled something on his notepad.

"The young man who sketched Anne's locket," Violet said. "What did he have to say about it?"

I looked at Whitlock, and he nodded, giving me the green light to share information about Logan.

"Logan is missing," I said.

"*Missing?*" Eugene said, setting a coffee mug down in front of Violet. "What do you mean?"

"No one has seen him in several days. Believe me, if I could talk to him, I would. I believe finding him is the key to solving Audrey's murder."

"Seems like you need to do it sooner than later."

"That we do." Whitlock closed his notepad and stood. "We'll leave you our numbers. If you remember anything else, any detail, call us."

Violet nodded, blotting her eyes with a tissue she pulled from her pocket.

Eugene walked us to the door, shaking his head as he said, "It's hard, you know? Thinking about the possibility of knowing what happened to Anne after all this time. I was resigned to the fact that we'd never know."

"I think we'll find answers," I said. "At least, my gut tells me we will."

Whitlock and I stepped onto the porch, and as the door closed behind us, Whitlock blew out a breath. "A truck. A man with a tattoo. A locket with Anne's name on it. A scarf that may provide further evidence ..."

"And two girls," I said. "One dead. And one still missing, presumably dead."

Whitlock opened the driver's side door and paused. "I think we may be looking at the same killer. A man who waited twenty-five years to strike again."

I nodded, because I believed he was right.

If both women had died by the same hand, then the killer had stepped out of the past and into the present, and there was no reason to believe they were finished killing yet.

17

Whitlock dropped me off at the house with a quick nod and a promise to stay in touch. Then he drove away, disappearing down the hill. I stood there for a moment, allowing the morning sun to warm my back as I thought through our conversation with Violet and Eugene.

We had learned a lot.

Violet's grandfather had built the cabin.

Her family owned the land where Audrey was murdered.

Around the time Anne went missing, they'd seen a man with a cross tattoo.

It was as if the cold case was refusing to stay cold, at long last.

I unlocked my vehicle, slid behind the wheel, and gave Giovanni a call. "Your car's not here."

"I'm in a meeting with our financial advisor," he said. "Is everything all right?"

"My visit with Violet and Eugene Fontaine is putting everything into perspective. Are you free for lunch?"

"I'm always free for lunch with you. Where would you like to go?"

"The Boathouse Diner."

"Ahh, one of our favorites. What time?"

"Thirty minutes?"

"I'll be there."

Twenty-five minutes later, I pulled into the restaurant parking lot. The Boathouse Diner sat near the edge of Main Street, tucked between a bait shop and a kayak rental company. Its weathered white siding and cobalt-blue trim had held strong against wind, salt, and sun for over three decades. The diner had started as an actual boathouse, owned by a retired fisherman named Billy Bob Armstrong, who had decided one day that he'd spent enough of his life hauling nets and wanted to serve up food instead.

Billy kept the original structure, reinforcing the walls with reclaimed ship planks, and he added a dining room in the back to serve more patrons. Rumor had it the brick fireplace in that room, my favorite part of the place, came from the home of Jeremiah Johnson, one of the town's earliest settlers and entrepreneurs. Tourists often stopped at the diner because of their clam chowder, which had been awarded one of the best in the state. But the locals came for Billy, a master storyteller who loved sharing his seafaring tales.

I exited the car and saw that Giovanni had parked a few spots down. Inside, the diner bustled with the late lunch crowd, and a jukebox was playing oldies near the bar area. The pleasant aroma of fresh cherry pie drifted through the air.

Billy stood behind the register, polishing a brass bell with a cloth. He was dressed in his usual sea-captain ensemble: navy peacoat, wool cap, trimmed white beard, and a posture that suggested he'd once spent more time on water than land.

He looked up and pointed the cloth at me like it was an extension of his hand.

"Ahoy, Georgiana, it's nice to see you."

"And you, Billy."

"It's been a while."

"We've been meaning to stop in. I believe Giovanni's already here?"

Billy motioned toward the back room. "By the fire, your favorite spot. Take a seat, and we'll catch up in a jiffy."

I nodded and walked past the main dining area, entering the back room, where the old brick fireplace framed the far wall. A small fire crackled in the hearth, giving off warmth that seeped into the wooden floorboards. Giovanni sat near the window. We embraced, and I joined him, my attention turning toward the kitchen as I studied the movement inside.

Pots clanged.

A spatula flipped something I couldn't see.

And every so often, a large silhouette moved in front of the stove.

"You seem to be watching the kitchen with intention," Giovanni said.

"I am."

He tapped a finger against my arm. "Are you going to tell me why?"

"In a minute."

The chef, a large man everyone called Bear, worked with a precision that surprised people when they first saw him. His shoulders were broad enough to block the kitchen doorway, and his thick, muscular arms looked as though he chopped firewood every morning before breakfast.

But that wasn't the reason I studied him.

Our waiter, a young teen who'd been hired several months earlier, approached with menus. "Welcome back. Can I get any drinks started for you?"

"Two iced teas," Giovanni said. "Unsweetened."

The waiter nodded and walked away with a promise to

return in a moment to take our order. Billy entered the room and walked over, brushing flour off his coat as he approached.

"Well, look at you two," he said with a smile. "Haven't seen you for a couple of months. Thought you ran off to Europe or someplace fancy."

Giovanni laughed, patting Billy on the shoulder. "I apologize we haven't been in for a while, my friend. We've been busy."

Billy leaned both hands on the edge of the table. "Busy is overrated. But I'm happy you're here. Got a new batch of sourdough today. I'll get your waiter to bring you some bread and butter in just a minute."

"Wonderful." I leaned in close, lowering my voice. "Hey, can I ask you a question?"

"Anything for you, darlin.'"

"It's about Bear."

"What about him?"

"How long has he worked for you?"

"Ever since I opened the place. He's like family to me. Why?"

"I've been looking into a cold case, and earlier this morning, someone described a man that reminded me a lot of him."

"He in some kind of trouble?"

"Not at all. I'd just like to ask him a couple of questions if you can spare him for a few minutes."

"Sure, sure. But knowing what you do, I feel I must put in a good word before I leave you." Turning toward the kitchen, he glanced at Bear. "That right there is one of the most stand-up gentlemen I've ever met. Sure, he looks a bit rough around the edges, but that's not always a good judge of character, is it?"

"It is not."

He nodded and walked away as the waiter returned with our drinks and a basket of bread. We gave him our order, and as he took it to the kitchen, Giovanni leaned in, saying, "At least I know why we're here today. What does Bear have to do with your case?"

"I'll explain everything when I get a chance to talk to him."

He took a sip of his tea. "So, you're keeping me in suspense."

I shot him a wink. "Babe, you live with a private investigator. Suspense comes with the territory."

Minutes later, the waiter returned with a bowl of clam chowder for Giovanni and a turkey club sandwich for me. Giovanni thanked him and reached for his spoon. As we ate, Billy sent over a few complimentary appetizers to the table, and we made small talk and enjoyed our feast. Every so often, I'd look up and notice Bear glancing at me, stone-faced. He looked nervous, or worried, or both.

He waited until we'd finished our meal, and then as the plates were removed from the table, he dried his hands on a towel and walked over.

"Everything okay with the food?" he asked.

"It was excellent, as usual."

He slid into the seat next to me, on a chair that was made for someone half his size. "You wanted to see me?"

I nodded and thought about what to say next. "Did you grow up here, in Cambria?"

"Born and raised."

"I wanted to ask you about your tattoo."

His attention shifted to his ankle, then back to me. "What about it?"

"When did you get it?"

He swallowed, and his jaw tightened. "I don't know. A long time ago."

"What does it symbolize?"

He shifted his weight from one foot to the other. "Why does this matter?"

"I'm just curious."

He cocked his head to one side. "I know you're a private detective. You're more than a little curious."

"I'll admit, I'm working on a case. This morning, I was speaking to Violet and Eugene Fontaine. Violet's daughter, Anne, went missing in Cambria twenty-five years ago. Around the time she disappeared, Anne and her Aunt Glinda saw a man in her aunt's neighborhood, a man whose description made me think of you. Same build. Same tattoo."

His lips parted, and I waited to hear what he had to say. But he didn't speak, at first.

"I don't want to talk about it here," he said. "Not at work, and not around a bunch of locals."

Giovanni leaned forward. "When do you finish work today?"

"Five."

"Why don't you come to our house after you get off? We can have a few drinks, and you and Georgiana can—"

"I don't drink. But yeah, I can do that." Bear hesitated, his gaze darting between us, a mix of fear, shame, and something that looked almost like relief. "What I tell you, it stays between us, right?"

"As long as there isn't a reason for it not to stay between us," I said.

He nodded once and stood, returning to the kitchen without another word.

"I wonder what he'll say when we see him this evening," Giovanni said.

"Me too."

I glanced outside as the wind began pushing against the windows, rattling the glass as if something old and buried was waking up. Whatever it was, I was ready for it to make its way to the surface.

18

Bear arrived at our house just past five, as the last of the daylight faded into a pale blue wash behind the pines. Luka barked once, offering a deep, territorial warning, until I cracked the door open. The moment Bear stepped into view, Luka's growl dissolved into an eager wiggle, as if Bear were an old friend.

"Well, that's a good sign," Giovanni murmured behind me.

Bear stood on the porch with his hands shoved into the pockets of his black shorts, which seemed an odd clothing choice given it was winter. For such a large man, he seemed unsure how to position himself as he shifted his weight every few seconds.

"Thanks for having me over," he said, "and for not pressing me to talk at the diner with all our customers around."

"You bet," I said. "Come on in."

He stepped into the foyer, pulling a knit beanie off his head and smoothing his hair with a palm as if trying to make himself presentable. He stood in polite discomfort, like a gentle giant who had crashed a tea party.

Giovanni gestured toward the den. "We've been relaxing in here tonight. Make yourself comfortable."

Bear ducked through the doorway and paused, taking in the room. A fire crackled in the fireplace, giving the space a cozy glow. On the coffee table was a cheese platter with crackers, olives, and a bowl of mixed nuts, sitting beside my glass of champagne and Giovanni's whisky.

Bear remained standing until Giovanni motioned toward the sofa.

"Please," Giovanni said, "sit."

Bear eased down.

The sofa creaked under his weight, though it held.

"You all right?" Giovanni asked.

Bear attempted a nod, but his twitching hands betrayed him.

"I don't want to intrude," he said. "And I don't want any trouble."

"You're not intruding," I said. "And you're not in trouble."

Luka wandered over, sniffed Bear's boot, then pressed his head against Bear's thigh with a soft grunt. Bear froze, then let out a deep breath.

"Huh," he said. "Guess he likes me."

"Luka knows good people," Giovanni replied, taking a seat on a chair beside me.

Bear gave Luka an awkward pat, and Luka responded by thumping his tail against the rug.

After a moment, Bear cleared his throat. "I know you offered to have me come over for a drink when you were at the diner, and I said no to the drink, but ... I wouldn't mind one now. If it's still all right."

"Of course," Giovanni said, rising. "Whisky?"

"Yes, please."

Giovanni poured a glass and handed it to him. Bear took a

sip, then another, his shoulders lowering as the warmth settled in.

"All right," he said. "Ask whatever you need to ask."

I folded my hands in my lap. "At the restaurant, I told you Glinda and Anne saw a man in their neighborhood right before Anne went missing, someone matching your description. Anne's mother, Violet, also saw a man sitting in a truck outside her sister's house, and she believes it was the same person. Was that man you?"

Bear stared into his glass, swirling the whisky once before answering. "Yes."

Giovanni sat back, absorbing what Bear had just admitted, though his expression remained calm.

"Why were you there?" I asked.

"It's a long story."

"We have time," I said.

Bear looked into the fire, the flames flickering across his face. "My mother died twenty-six years ago," he said. "Before she passed, she told me something she'd kept secret for most of her life. She said I deserved to know the truth."

"The truth about what?" I asked.

"She told me that Violet and Glinda's father ... well, she said he was my father too."

I exchanged a glance with Giovanni but remained silent.

"My mother told me she and their father had an affair decades ago," he said. "It wasn't long-term. It wasn't serious. Just one of those things that shouldn't have happened but did."

"Before she told you the truth, who did you believe your father to be?"

"The man who raised me. He came into the picture when my mother was pregnant. I thought it was strange, the fact he was so small and, well, I'm not, but I never questioned it."

"Did Violet and Glinda's father know about you?"

"Doubt it. My mother said she never told him."

"I assume that's the reason you were seen at Glinda's house all those years ago," I said.

He nodded. "I just wanted to … I don't know … I wanted to see them, to see where I came from and if they looked like me. I never knew they were worried about who I was, but I understand now why they would be."

"How often were you in Glinda's neighborhood?"

"It was just a few times," Bear admitted. "I thought maybe I'd get the courage to knock on the door and introduce myself. But then Anne went missing, and everyone panicked. I realized it wasn't the right moment to show up and say, 'Hey, I might be your half-brother.'"

"And then Anne was never found."

"She wasn't, and after the dust settled and the years passed, it felt too late to step into their lives, so I kept the truth to myself. Aside from my mother and the man who raised me, Billy is the only other person who knows the truth."

"That's why he put in a good word for you today," Giovanni said.

Bear nodded. "He's a decent man."

I studied him, thinking about what to say next. "Did you ever have any interaction with Anne?"

"No, I never spoke to her, and we never met. Like I said, I wasn't in that neighborhood often, and when I was, I kept to myself. When she went missing, I felt sick for the family, but believe me when I say I had nothing to do with that girl's disappearance."

I believed him.

Every word.

Nothing about what he just said was deceptive. He seemed like a man with past regrets, a man who lived alone with a truth he didn't know how to share.

"Do you have any idea what happened to Anne?" I asked.

"None," he said. "If I did, I would have told someone long ago. I know what it feels like to lose family. I wouldn't let someone else go through that if I could help them out somehow."

Bear was a dead end, but I found myself satisfied that it turned out the way it had. His story didn't solve Anne's disappearance or Audrey's murder, but it filled in another part of the puzzle.

The cabin.

The land.

The family connection.

A man who belonged to the same bloodline but lived outside it.

Bear shifted in his seat, setting the empty glass on the side table. "I should go. I've already taken up enough of your evening."

"You can stay for as long as you need," Giovanni said.

Bear shook his head, rising. "Thank you for listening."

I stood as well. "Bear, there's something I'd like you to consider before you leave. Violet has lost a sister and a daughter. Don't you think she deserves the chance to know her family, even if it's someone coming into her life whom she didn't expect?"

He froze, placing his hand on the back of the sofa.

"You don't have to tell her now," I said, "and you don't ever have to tell her. But she might welcome the chance to get to know you. People find strength in connection, even when the past is complicated."

"I'll think about it."

"If you decide to let her know, I'd be happy to make the introductions."

He offered me a small, pained smile and walked to the door,

Luka trailing after him. After he left, Giovanni cleared the glasses and plates, and we extinguished the fire and headed to bed.

But tonight, sleep felt far away.

There were too many scattered pieces.

Too many shadows.

Too many unanswered questions.

I lay in bed staring at the ceiling, replaying Violet's trembling voice, Bear's confession, and the echo of Anne's name which seemed to be at every turn.

I needed clarity, and I knew where I intended to find it tomorrow, at Rosemary Ashford's house. I'd update her on the case and then ask to search Audrey's room. Somewhere inside that room I hoped to find a clue, one Audrey never had the chance to share. A clue that might help me understand what happened to Anne and what led to Audrey's death.

19

As I pulled into the Ashfords' driveway the next morning, a light glowed in the kitchen window, and for a moment, I saw silhouettes moving inside.

I'd called the night before to ask Rosemary if I could come by. She'd agreed without hesitation.

I stepped out of the car and walked up the drive. Before I reached the porch, the door opened, and Rosemary waved me inside, saying, "Come in, Georgiana. We've just made breakfast, and you're welcome to join us. There's plenty."

"It smells incredible," I said, stepping inside.

The scent of pancakes and bacon lingered in the air, mixing with the faint sweetness of maple syrup. As we entered the kitchen, I saw a man I assumed to be Rosemary's husband at the stove, turning bacon with slow, deliberate movements. His tall, thin frame made me wonder whether he'd lost weight since the death of his daughter or if he'd always looked that way.

He turned, offering me a slight smile. "You must be Georgiana."

"I am."

"I'm Dustin, Rosemary's husband."

"Good to meet you. Thank you for letting me come by."

He nodded, then began putting strips of bacon onto a plate, and I sat down at the table, which had already been set with pancakes stacked on a platter, eggs in a ceramic bowl, and a pitcher of orange juice.

Rosemary poured a glass for each of us and took a seat beside me.

"I'm glad you're here," she said. "We could use a more detailed update."

Dustin sat beside her, his hands clasped together, eyes fixed on the table. He glanced at me for a brief moment, the pain in his eyes laying bare the weight he was carrying.

"What have you found out?" he asked.

I took a breath. "I don't have a lot of answers for you yet, but I am getting somewhere."

In unison, they leaned forward, anxious to hear what more I had to say.

"I've spoken to several people since I took this case, including the police, Logan's parents, some of Audrey's class-mates, and a few others. There's something I'd like to tell you, but if I do, I need you to agree to keep it to yourselves for now."

"Of course," Rosemary said.

"In one of Logan's sketchbooks, he drew a picture of a locket with the name *Anne* on it," I said. "It turns out Anne was a young woman who went missing twenty-five years ago."

Dustin raised a brow but said nothing.

"Why do you think he drew a sketch of a locket belonging to a woman who's been missing for so long?" Rosemary asked.

"Yesterday, I spoke with Anne's parents. They showed me a photo of Anne wearing the locket, and I confirmed it's the same one from Logan's sketchbook. And there's something else. Anne went missing while she was visiting her aunt in Cambria, who just so happened to live in the same subdivision you live in now."

Rosemary glanced at Dustin, then back at me. "I'm sorry to hear about the woman who went missing, but what does any of this have to do with our daughter?"

"It seems to me that Audrey found Anne's locket, and when she did, I bet she tried to figure out who owned it. My guess is that she discovered Anne went missing all those years ago. She told Logan, and the two of them may have done some investigating of their own. I believe digging up the past is what led to Audrey being murdered."

Dustin went pale, staring down at his hands. "Does this mean she was targeted?"

"I'm exploring the possibility. If I'm right, Audrey's death is connected to Anne."

They both went quiet, as if taking in what I'd just said. The silence was uncomfortable and heavy, but I understood the need for them to process everything. We finished our food with minimal small talk, and Rosemary rose to clear the plates.

I stood.

"Would it be all right if I spent a few minutes in Audrey's room?" I asked.

She hesitated a moment, then nodded. "The police have already searched it, but sure, if you think it will help."

Dustin pushed his chair back, rubbing the back of his neck. "I haven't been in there since she died. Can't bring myself to go inside."

Rosemary reached for his hand. "Stay down here if you need to, dear. I'll show Georgiana to Audrey's room."

He nodded and Rosemary led me upstairs to Audrey's room, pausing at the door before opening it.

"I guess you can say I'm the opposite of my husband," she

said, flicking away a few tears. "I've been in here every day, but I haven't touched a thing. It's just the way she left it."

She opened the door and stepped aside.

I walked in, getting the immediate sense that the room felt frozen in time. The walls were painted a soft purple, and there was a full-size bed with a gray comforter and a knitted blanket that was folded at the end of the bed. Miniature Polaroids were strung across the headboard—laughing faces, forest trails, snapshots of moments past.

A dresser sat beneath a round mirror and taped to the glass was a sketch of Audrey and Logan inside a heart, their initials overlapping where the lines met. The sketch held a simple sweetness, and yet it twisted my insides at the same time.

Two young people in love, a love that would never grow to fruition.

"I'm guessing Logan drew this of the two of them," I said.

Rosemary stepped beside me, her hand pressed to her chest. "She loved that drawing. She stuck it here the day he gave it to her."

"It's beautiful," I said. "Would you mind if I had a few minutes in her room alone? It's part of my process."

"Of course. Take all the time you need. I'll be downstairs with Dustin if you need anything."

She left the room, leaving me in the quiet of Audrey's space.

I started with the dresser. Each drawer held folded clothes, organized in a way that suggested Rosemary helped her keep it tidy. Nothing looked out of place. I checked beneath the clothes, inside pockets, behind the drawers, still seeing nothing of note.

I moved to the desk. The surface held notebooks, gel pens, and a single photo strip of Audrey and Talia making faces. I checked the drawers, flipped through the notebooks, and scanned pages of homework and doodles.

Still nothing.

Next, I moved to the bed. I lifted the mattress and checked beneath it, feeling along the slats as I searched under the frame. But again, I found nothing helpful. Nothing to help me solve her murder.

I looked through her nightstand, her closet, her shoes, even the tiny jewelry box on the dresser. No clues. Whitlock and Foley had done a thorough job when they were here.

Frustrated and left without a single clue, I stepped back, my hands on my hips as I studied the room one last time. Something tugged at me, an instinct telling me I was missing something that should have been obvious but wasn't.

Then my gaze drifted toward the window.

A small potted plant sat on the sill, its soil dry, leaves curled at the edges. I wondered if it had died before Audrey did, or if Rosemary had neglected to water it after her daughter passed.

I walked over to it and lifted the pot.

It felt light, almost *too* light.

I set it on the desk and attempted to separate the pot from its saucer, but it didn't budge at first. It was as if it had been taped or glued together, but not well. I pulled on the saucer again, and this time, it broke free. A small baggie was taped to the underside of the pot. I pulled off the baggie and opened it, reaching inside. As I removed its contents, my pulse quickened, and I froze, staring down at the silver locket in my hand—oval, delicate, and etched with a ring of tiny hearts.

In the center, a name: *Anne.*

Foley and Whitlock had missed it, though I understood why.

And Rosemary had never known to look.

Audrey had hidden it well.

I closed my hand around the locket, and a chill swept across my spine—a truth I couldn't shake. I was now certain someone had murdered Audrey to keep their secret buried, and I was closing in.

20

I arrived at the San Luis Obispo Police Department just before noon, the locket tucked inside an envelope in my coat pocket. The winter air clung to me as I stepped outside. I walked to the department, pulling open the glass doors as I headed toward Foley's office.

Whitlock stood in front of Foley's desk when I entered, one hand on his hip, the other drumming against a stack of files, as he hummed a familiar jazz tune. Foley sat at his computer, typing something, maybe a report.

Both men looked up at me at the same time, as if surprised to see me.

"I have something for you," I said, gripping the envelope.

Whitlock perked up. "Please tell me you found a winning lottery ticket."

I laughed. "This may be even better."

He reached for the envelope, and when I handed it over, he gave it a light shake. "What is it?"

I nodded at it. "Open it."

Whitlock tore the seal and peered inside, the color draining from his face as he stared at the locket.

"Well, what is it?" Foley asked.

Whitlock reached into his pocket, removing a glove, which he then slid on his hand. He pulled out the silver locket, holding it between his thumb and forefinger.

Foley stood so fast his chair rolled back, bumping the wall.

"You're joking," Foley said. "Is that what I think it is?"

"Anne Fontaine's locket."

"Where did you find it?"

"In Audrey's bedroom," I said.

Whitlock let out a slow breath. "Oh, for crying out ... *where?*"

"Inside a small bag taped between the bottom of a plant pot and a saucer. I only found it because I was fixating on the plant, trying to decide if it had died before or after Audrey did."

Foley rubbed his jaw.

"We checked that room top to bottom. The plant was making its exit when we saw it. Had only one green leaf left." He glanced at me, looking sheepish. "I should have found that locket. I should have known to look there. Teenagers hide things in strange places sometimes."

"You searched that room with the weight of a fresh murder on your back," I said. "Trust me, I almost left without checking the plant. It was hidden well. It's clear Audrey intended for it to stay out of sight."

Whitlock grabbed an evidence bag, and as he slipped the locket into the bag, it caught the light, and I saw something.

"Hold on," I said, leaning in for a closer look.

Whitlock paused. "What is it?"

"Look at the clasp." I pointed.

Foley crouched beside me. "Is that—"

"A hair," I said.

A single dark strand was caught in the tiny hinge, almost invisible until the light had hit it.

Foley's expression turned grim, and he said, "We know this is Anne's locket. Still, we need Silas."

"Yeah, we do," I said.

Foley grabbed his phone and made the call.

"Silas? Need you in the bullpen. Evidence." The call ended, and he turned toward me. "I'm sure we can all agree that Audrey didn't stumble into trouble. She found something that put her in someone's crosshairs."

"Someone with a reason to keep a secret in the past," Whitlock added.

Ten minutes later, Silas stepped through the doorway, his hair wild, tropical button-up shirt half tucked in, as if he'd been dragged away from something tedious.

Foley pointed at the locket, and Silas said, "What's this, then?"

"This here is a piece of history," Whitlock said.

"It's also evidence," Foley replied. "And there's a hair on it."

"I'm guessing it has to do with the investigation you're working on and the cold case Whitlock's looking into again?"

"It does," I said.

Whitlock had told Silas about Anne when he'd dropped off the scarf, but he wasn't sure how it was all connected. Over the next few minutes, I filled Silas in on the locket, its connection to Anne Fontaine, and to the abandoned cabin.

"Speaking of the cabin," Silas said, "I've been wanting to talk to you about that."

"What do you know?" Foley asked.

Silas reached into his bag and pulled out a small plastic container holding the vertebrae I recovered and set it on the desk between us.

"It's human," he said.

Whitlock closed his eyes for a second, his expression a

mixture of relief and sadness over what it meant. If the bone was human, we might be solving two murders, not one.

"Which part of the spine is it from?" Foley asked.

"Thoracic vertebrae," Silas said. "Midback."

He tapped the side of the container. "Based on the morphology, I believe it belonged to a female."

Foley raised a brow. "How can you tell?"

"Male vertebrae tend to be thicker and heavier," Silas said. "Female vertebrae show subtle differences, lower down the spine where curvature helps accommodate childbirth. This one aligns with female anatomy. Not definitive yet, but I'm close enough to make the call."

I felt a knot in my stomach. "I wonder if it's Anne's."

"It's possible," Silas said. "I can't confirm until we compare DNA. But the locket? The hair? The bone? Something tells me you're headed in the right direction."

"I wonder if there are more remains at the cabin," I said.

"We were over there again yesterday. Didn't find anything more, though we haven't done any digging yet."

"If the bone is Anne's, what you found is just the beginning," Foley said. "That bone wasn't sitting there for twenty-five years without company. I'll call the judge, let him know we need a warrant to dig at the cabin."

Whitlock nodded.

Silas gathered up the locket and the bone and placed both in his bag. "I'll go ahead and test the strand of hair, even though we're just almost certain that it's Anne's."

He left the room, and Foley reached for his coat. "If that cabin holds the rest of Anne's remains, we need to get to it fast, before the killer has another chance to clean up the past."

21

Foley texted me an hour later saying the judge was reviewing the warrant.

"Shouldn't be much longer," he added. "Be ready."

Ready felt like an understatement.

I decided to use the time the way Whitlock always did when he was waiting on something, and to squeeze whatever fruit was left on the tree.

When I'd spoken to Audrey's classmate Sadie about the party, the purse, and the missing money, she'd told me Willow Robinson knew Logan better than most. If anyone knew where he'd gone, or if he was safe, it might be her. And I'd been meaning to talk to her anyway.

I headed toward the Robinson house, and when I arrived and knocked on the door, footsteps sounded inside, heavy ones at first, then lighter ones behind. When the door opened, a tall, broad man with a dark beard and a stiff posture stood in the doorway. His arms were crossed as if he was expecting trouble.

"Does Willow Robinson live here?" I asked.

"Who's asking?"

"Are you Aiden?"

He nodded. "Again, who's asking?"

"I'm Georgiana Germaine, a private investigator working with the police on Audrey Ashford's case."

His grip on the door tightened. "We're not interested in talking to you about the case. It's got nothin' to do with us."

Before he had a chance to close the door, a gentle voice drifted from behind. "Dad, wait. It's all right. I want to talk to her."

Willow stepped into view, and the tension shifted. She was slender with soft brown hair pulled into a loose ponytail, and there was a sweetness about her, a calm presence that drew me in.

"*Dad*," Willow said. "Let her in."

He shot her a look that said he didn't think it was a wise idea, but after a long moment, he stepped aside. "You can come inside as long as you understand I'm staying in the room while you talk to my daughter."

"I understand," I said, though it made things trickier than I'd hoped.

The house was warm but cluttered when I walked in, with mismatched furniture and a faint smell of sawdust. Aiden led us into the living room, where he took a seat in the armchair. Willow sat on the couch. I remained standing.

"Thank you for agreeing to speak with me," I said to Willow.

She nodded. "I want to help. Audrey was my friend. We were supposed to spend the weekend together, a group of us. On the day she died, Audrey asked me to come over to help finalize plans with her and Talia, but I told her to make the decisions without me. If I'd been there ... maybe things would be different now."

Aiden cleared his throat. "No sense thinking that way, Willow."

"I'm not blaming myself," she said. "I just miss her."

"Sounds like you and Audrey were good friends," I said.

Willow nodded. "She was easy to be around, and we were a lot alike in personality. She didn't always tell people what she was dealing with, though. She kept a lot inside."

Aiden tugged at his beard. "Why do you need to know all this information? The police have already questioned Willow. This house is not a revolving door for questions."

"I'm trying to fill in the gaps," I said. "There are things Audrey may have known that put her in danger."

Willow looked up quickly, alarm touching her face. "What things?"

Again, Aiden cut in. "Maybe it's best we don't know. Don't need to be getting all caught up in whatever got her killed."

"Dad!"

"It's the truth, isn't it?" he shot back.

"I want to know."

And I wanted to be as far away as I could from this guy.

"Ask your questions," Aiden said, "but keep 'em simple."

It wasn't the ideal situation, but I'd take what I could get.

"All right," I said, turning toward Willow. "You spent time with Audrey. Did she ever mention feeling unsafe? Or did she tell you about anything strange she might have found? Or a secret she may have been keeping?"

Willow hesitated, then shook her head. "No. At least not to me."

Aiden nodded, satisfied.

"What about Logan?" I asked.

Willow's expression shifted—not much, but enough for me to notice she'd stiffened.

"Logan?" she repeated.

"You're close friends with him, right?"

She glanced at her father, then back at me. "I guess so."

"He's missing," I said. "No one has heard from him in days."

I studied Willow's face, noting the news I'd just told her didn't seem to come as a shock.

Aiden leaned forward. "Logan is a strange kid. You shouldn't waste time on him."

Willow gave him a frustrated glance.

"He isn't strange," she said. "People say things about him that aren't fair. He keeps to himself, but he's a good person."

"Do you know where he is now?" I asked.

Her breath caught, almost imperceptible, but enough to expose her.

She *knew* something.

But she remained quiet.

"Willow, if you know where Logan is, I can help him if he's in trouble. I can protect him a lot better than he can protect himself."

Aiden looked at his daughter, then at me. "That's enough questions. You have no right coming in here and implying my daughter knows something about the kid's whereabouts."

"I'm not implying anything," I said. "I'm trying to find him, to make sure he's safe."

"Good luck with that," he said. "We're done here."

Aiden shot up, standing in front of me like a blockade.

I reached into my coat pocket and pulled out a card, handing it to Willow. "If you think of anything I should know, anything at all, please get in touch with me. And I meant what I said about Logan. I can protect him. I'm not here to get him in trouble. I'm here to get him out of it."

Willow reached for the card, but Aiden snatched it instead.

"She won't be getting in touch," he said.

He glanced out the window, eyes wide as he cursed at a car parking in front of his house, which gave me just enough time to reach into my pocket again, pulling out a second card. I slipped it into Willow's hand.

"Time for you to go, Detective."

I stepped through the doorway, and before I reached the porch step, the door slammed behind me so hard the frame rattled.

I walked to my car with the heavy certainty that Willow was hiding something, not about Audrey, but about Logan.

And then there was Aiden, whose defensiveness felt excessive. Whether that was his nature or a sign of something deeper, I wasn't sure.

I slid into the driver's seat, turned the ignition, and rested my hands on the wheel. Then my phone lit up with an unknown number.

This is Willow.
I know where Logan is, but please don't tell my dad.
I'll send the address.

A few seconds later, a drop pin appeared, and my heart raced.

Logan wasn't just missing.

He was hiding.

And whatever he knew, it was time I heard his side of the story.

All of it.

22

After a quick stop at home to change into more outdoorsy attire, I left the house, hopeful I'd find Logan and get him to talk. Willow's pin took me to the Lost Prairie Wilderness, a rugged stretch of land about an hour from Cambria. It was best known for its high, jagged peaks and oak woodlands, which wound around a conifer forest. If Logan was trying not to be found, it was the perfect place to hide.

I drove until the road narrowed to a single lane, and when pavement gave way to dirt, I parked and continued on foot. Stepping out of the car, I breathed in a mixture of sunbaked sage and damp soil.

As I made my way deeper into the area, the wind worked through the branches above me, rattling them like bones.

After almost an hour of walking, I spotted a tent half hidden behind a cluster of scrub oak, set beside a pickup truck. The truck matched the one seen in the gas station's surveillance video. The tent's faded blue fabric sagged on one side, as though the pole meant to support it had just about given out.

I approached the tent with caution, listening for any sounds coming from the inside, but there weren't any. When I reached the opening, I crouched down and peeled the flap back, peeking inside. A sleeping bag lay twisted near the back next to a stack of protein bar wrappers. But what stood out the most was what appeared to be dried blood along the tent flap near the zipper.

It wasn't much.

But it was something.

If Logan had been staying here, he wasn't here now.

Hoping he was nearby, I backed away from the tent and turned, shouting, "Logan Lambert? My name is Georgiana Germaine, and I'm a private investigator. If you're in trouble, I'm here to help."

My words were met with silence.

I tried again.

"Logan, I know you're out here. Please, I just want to talk."

It felt like my words fell into the open air, and then I heard it. The sound of footsteps—someone running.

I glanced around and caught a flash of movement, a young man sprinting through the trees, heading uphill.

"Logan, wait!" I shouted.

When it became clear he wasn't going to stop, I chased after him, branches slapping at my arms as I navigated the terrain. He was fast, but in his panic to get away, his foot caught on a root, and he stumbled, giving me the chance to catch up.

At first I thought he'd jump back up and take off again, but he didn't. He turned, looking up at me with sad eyes, as if accepting defeat.

His face was gaunt and smeared with dirt, his T-shirt stiff with sweat and grime. His eyes were red and raw from what I assumed was a lack of sleep, and one finger was wrapped in a bandage.

"Why did you run?" I asked.

The truth was, I knew why he had.

He didn't know me or the reason why I was there.

He shrugged. "I don't know. It seemed like the right thing to do."

"All I ask is that you hear me out and allow me to explain who I am and why I'm here. All right?"

"Guess so."

"I was hired by Audrey Ashford's mother to investigate her murder."

He flinched at her name but said nothing.

"I saw the sketches you made of Anne's locket," I continued. "And yesterday, I found the locket in Audrey's room."

"You did?"

I nodded. "I'm guessing Audrey found that locket either in the abandoned cabin in the woods near her house, or somewhere nearby. She showed it to you, and the two of you did some research and figured out a girl named Anne went missing twenty-five years ago. Am I right?"

"So far."

I pointed at his hand. "What happened?"

"I was trying to cut a bag open with my pocketknife and nicked my finger."

It explained the blood I saw on the tent flap.

"Are you out here because you're worried the person who murdered Audrey might target you next?" I asked.

"Yeah, but I don't know anything. At least, I don't think I do."

"The killer might not be aware of that."

"No kidding. Why do you think I'm out here?"

I moved a hand to my hip. "What is your plan, anyway? You can't stay out here forever."

"I don't have one. I just knew I had to get away, somewhere I could think." He dragged the back of his hand across his forehead, smearing more dirt on his skin. "I can't go back. If they find me—"

"They won't," I said. "You may not have a plan, but I do."

"What is it?"

"Until I solve this case, you can stay with me."

He blinked at me like he was unsure he'd heard me right. "With you? I don't even know you."

"And I don't know you, but you can trust me. Why don't we pack up everything, and you can follow me back to my house?"

"I ... ahh, my truck won't start. Before you got here, I was planning to hike my way out of here."

"All right, new plan. Let's leave the truck for now. We'll come back for it later."

He gave the suggestion some thought. "How do you plan on keeping me safe?"

"My husband and I have private security. Not a home system. An actual guard on our property."

I left out the part about Giovanni needing security because he came from a world much different than the world he was living in now, with me.

I reached out, and he took my hand, and I helped him up.

"My mom won't be okay with me staying with you," he said.

"Oh, I agree. I've met her. How old are you?"

"Eighteen."

"Well then, whether your mother likes the idea or not, it's not her decision. It's yours," I said. "You're old enough to decide for yourself. So, what do you say?"

He offered me a slight smile, his expression starting to ease.

It was a start.

"Come on," I said, placing a hand on his shoulder. "Let's get you out of the wilderness, fed and showered.

He hesitated a second, and then he nodded.
And for me, that was enough.

23

The ride back from Lost Prairie Wilderness was quiet—not awkward, just heavy. Logan stared out the passenger window for most of the drive, his fingers picking at the dirt beneath his nails.

As we drove into town, he cleared his throat and looked at me. "Hey, can I use your phone? Mine's dead."

"Of course," I said, unlocking it and handing it to him.

He tapped in a number, and the call rang once before someone answered, loud enough for me to hear what they were saying on the other end.

"Logan? Where are you? Are you safe? Why haven't you—"

"I'm safe, Mom," he said, cutting her off. "I'm not coming home yet though."

"What do you mean you're not ... Logan, you listen to me right now. We've been beside ourselves wondering where you are. I want you to come straight home. You have a lot of explaining to do."

"I know. We can talk more later. You and Dad don't need to worry. I'm okay."

"Tell me where you are."

"I gotta go. I'm sorry."

"Logan, please—"

He sighed, ending the call before she had the chance to say anything more, pressing the phone to his chest and closing his eyes.

I gave him some time, and then I said, "You know, you don't have to hide what's happened from your mother. It's been days since she's heard from you, and while she seems like a tough woman, you're her son. I can't imagine how worried she is right now."

"I know," he whispered. "But I know her. If I tell her what I told you, she won't let me out of her sight."

I decided not to push him further. Right now, he needed food, clean clothes, a shower, and to feel safe and supported.

We pulled into the driveway, then Logan followed me inside the house, Luka bounding up with an enthusiastic bark that made Logan jump. He took a moment to steady himself and then reached down, giving Luka a quick pat.

"Come on in and make yourself comfortable."

He nodded, lingering just inside the doorway, as if unsure whether to step farther into the house.

I waved him in. "Come on, I'll point you to the kitchen, and you can get yourself something to drink."

We made our way to the kitchen, and I opened the refrigerator door. "Take anything you want. I'll be right back."

I found Giovanni in the study. He glanced up when I entered and smiled.

"Well," he said, leaning back, "did you find the boy?"

"I did."

"Is he all right?"

"He will be."

I filled Giovanni in on the latest, and when I finished, he crossed his arms.

"You made the right decision bringing him here. No one will touch him while he's in this house."

I smiled. "I knew you'd say that."

He brushed past me into the hall, like he'd switched into host mode, peeking into the kitchen where Logan sat at the table.

"Let's get him into the shower and find him a change of clothes," I said. "Then we'll feed him. He's so skinny, if a stiff breeze came along, it would knock him right over."

While Giovanni grabbed a few things out of the closet, I led Logan to the guest room and showed him how to use the en-suite shower. Giovanni brought in several clothing options, which were oversized but would work for tonight.

We left him to get cleaned up, following the aroma of Giovanni's spaghetti carbonara back to the kitchen. Logan joined us several minutes later, looking nervous, his hands clasped together, eyes darting around like he was about to be interrogated.

Which, to be fair, he would be.

But not yet.

Giovanni set a bowl of pasta in front of him, and I said, "Why don't we eat dinner first and then talk after?"

Logan nodded, and when we joined him at the table, I guided the conversation elsewhere. Talking about Giovanni's day, instead of Logan's, seemed to help him relax.

Once dinner was finished, Logan and I moved to the den.

"Logan," I began, "I don't want to overwhelm you, but I still feel like I am trying to put together all the parts of the story. If you're up for it, I'd appreciate it if you could start at the beginning. Why did you run? And what do you know about Anne and about what happened to Audrey and why?"

He drew in a breath, holding it for a moment. "It all started at the cabin. Audrey loved hanging out there. If she and her mother argued, she'd go there to cool off. That's not to say they had a bad relationship. It was just normal mother-daughter stuff."

I crossed one leg over the other. "You said it all started at the cabin. I'm guessing something happened one day when she was there?"

"Yeah, she found that locket. It was stuck between a couple of planks on the floor next to the bed. She wouldn't have ever seen it, except she pulled the bed out one day to sweep behind it, and that's when she made her first discovery."

"I'm guessing there was a second discovery?"

"I'll get to that in a minute. After she found the locket, she showed it to me. At first, we didn't think much of it. But then she started searching the internet, and that's how we learned about Anne."

"What did she find out?"

He rubbed his forehead. "She came across some old articles about a woman named Anne Fontaine who'd disappeared from here. She also found a photo of a missing persons flyer, and in it, Anne was wearing the locket."

"And Audrey made the connection."

"Yeah, but it went way beyond that," he said. "Audrey became obsessed with what happened to Anne. I told her she needed to drop it, and she'd told me she'd let it go, but she didn't. She kept digging, looking for information on anyone who lived in Cambria back then. She thought someone local might have killed Anne. Someone who still lives here now."

"What else did Audrey find out?" I asked.

He paused, then said, "One night we were at a party, and she was acting a lot different than usual."

"Different how?"

"She believed someone knew she was digging into the case, but she didn't know who. She said she wasn't safe, and she was afraid I wasn't either. I told her she either needed to go to the police or to drop it and leave it alone for a while. She thought it was time to involve the police, but then she was murdered."

"Why didn't you go to the police?"

"I didn't know where the locket was, and I wanted to find it first," he said. "I thought it might be in her room, so I went to her parents one day and asked if I could spend some time there. They agreed. I never found it."

"I did."

Logan glared at me, shocked. "You did? Where?"

"Stuck between the bottom of a planter and its saucer. I took it to the police, and we found a strand of hair caught inside. They're testing it now."

"Maybe her death ... maybe it won't all be for nothing," he said, wiping a tear from his eye.

"It won't be," I said. "I'll make sure of it."

"I know I told you I left town because I thought someone might come after me, and I did. It's just ... I don't *think* someone is after me, I *know* they are."

I leaned forward. "Go on."

"A few weeks after Audrey died, I found a note on my truck. I'll show you. Be right back."

He left the room, returning a minute later, reaching into his dirty, half-zipped backpack, and pulling out a crumpled slip of paper. He smoothed it over the best he could and then handed it to me.

LEAVE THE PAST BURIED OR YOU'LL END UP JUST LIKE HER

I swore under my breath.

"And you didn't go to the police?" I asked.

Logan shook his head. "I didn't trust anyone. Not after what happened. If someone killed Audrey to hide a secret, then that someone could be anyone in this town. Anyone with power. Anyone with a badge. *Anyone.*"

Giovanni entered the room, taking a seat next to me. "You're safe here with us, and you're welcome to stay here for as long as it takes to solve this case."

"He's right," I added. "But now that you're with us, I want you to be straight with us about everything from here on out. No more half-truths."

He went quiet for a time, and then said, "The place I've been camping, I took Audrey there a couple of times. The last time I spoke to her, she referred to it as our safe place, a place where secrets go to hide."

Before I could respond, a sharp knock rattled the front door —loud, urgent, and unexpected.

Logan froze.

Giovanni stood, his jaw tight, eyes narrowing—not alarmed, just alert.

Old habits.

Old instincts.

Then he made his way down the hall to greet our unexpected visitor.

24

A low voice drifted from the foyer, followed by Giovanni's warmer one. A second later, Marco, our security guard, stepped into view behind Giovanni, carrying a tin wrapped in red cellophane.

He gave me a polite nod. "Evening. One of your neighbors dropped this off," he said, holding up the tin. "Holiday cookies. Figured I'd hand them over instead of leaving them on your front porch."

"Thank you, Marco," I said.

"Of course," he said. "You all have a good night."

Logan exhaled so hard his shoulders slumped forward. "I thought ... I don't know what I thought."

"You'll get used to Marco," Giovanni said, returning to his seat. "He watches this house like a hawk. Nothing gets past him."

It was meant to reassure, and it seemed to work.

Giovanni excused himself to gather the dishes, and Logan and I lowered ourselves back into the chairs beside the hearth. "All right. You told me about Audrey, what she found out at the cabin, and her being worried someone knew she was digging into the past. What did she think happened to Anne?"

"She thought Anne was murdered. And she was convinced it had been covered up."

I leaned forward. "Covered up by who?"

Logan shook his head. "She didn't know. That was the problem. She had all these ideas. I didn't know whether they were crazy or legit."

"Tell me about her ideas."

"She thought a local was involved. Someone her parents may have gone to school with back then, or someone who'd lived near Anne's aunt. She made a list of people who lived in the Harvest Creek neighborhood during that time and then cross-referenced them online to see who still lived in the area."

I was impressed.

This girl had been doing solid investigative work.

I was just disappointed it led to her demise.

"Did she suspect anyone more than others?" I asked.

His face tightened. "I don't know. If she did, she never gave me a name."

As the fire cracked in the background, I sat quiet for a moment, thinking about all the information he'd given me.

"Where were you when the note was left on your truck?" I asked.

"I skipped school that day. I couldn't be there anymore. Couldn't bear to see all the sorry faces of my classmates who didn't seem to know what to say to me. I drove to the park, just to think. I got out of my truck, walked around. When I got back to it, there was a note under the wiper. That's when I realized Audrey was right. Someone knew she was looking into Anne's disappearance."

I leaned back, letting the weight of his words settle, and then I remembered something about the conversation we were having before we were interrupted by the knock at the front door.

"Earlier, you were saying the last time you spoke to Audrey she mentioned Lost Prairie being a place secrets go to hide. What do you think she meant by that?"

"It's the reason I decided to go there, to see if what she'd said was more than just a random comment."

"And?"

"We made a rock pile out there once—you know those smooth, flat rocks that are balanced on top of each other?"

"I believe I know what you're talking about."

"When I got to the campsite several days ago, I noticed the rock pile had been changed. The rocks weren't stacked on top of each other anymore. They were piled up in a circle." He reached into his bag again, this time pulling out a dirty plastic bag. "I found this under the pile."

He held it out, and I stood, walking over to get a better look.

At first, it was hard to tell what the bag contained.

Then Logan offered some insight. "I think it's a bone."

"It looks like part of a pelvis," I said. "Do you know anything more about it?"

"I don't."

"Giovanni and I went to the cabin, and I found a small piece of bone. The coroner has confirmed it's human. I think there's a good chance this bone came from the same place we found the other one. The chief of police is trying to get a warrant to dig up the place. I'll be hearing from him soon."

Silence drifted through the room, warm but tense. It was as we were staring at the same puzzle, only now realizing which pieces fit and which didn't yet.

But it was coming together.

"I mean, it would be great to solve Anne's murder too, I

guess," he said, handing me the bag. "I just wish it could have been solved without Audrey losing her life."

"Yeah, me too."

Outside, the wind brushed against the windows, a soft hiss through the eaves as my phone buzzed on the coffee table.

It was a text message from Foley.

Warrant approved.
We're digging at the cabin in the morning.
Be ready.

I looked up at Giovanni, who'd just entered the room.

Then at Logan.

And at the firelight flickering across the walls.

Tomorrow, I had the feeling the case was going to break open, in one way or another.

25

I drove to the Lamberts' house midmorning, the clouds hanging low over Cambria like they couldn't decide whether to break or linger. As I was leaving, Logan was enjoying one of Giovanni's big breakfasts, and the two were talking about hockey, a passion it was clear they both shared. At one point, Logan even managed a slight laugh. I hadn't told Logan where I was going when I slipped out, deciding it would be better to tell him after the fact.

I parked at the curb and sat a moment before getting out, thinking about the reception I was about to receive. Part of me thought about driving away and letting Logan reach out to his parents again when he was ready. The other part knew how much they must be worrying about their son. Stopping by seemed like the right thing to do.

Tilly opened the door as soon as I knocked, her posture rigid, shoulders square like she'd been bracing for impact.

"What are *you* doing here?" she asked.

Her eyes flicked past me, scanning the yard, the street, my car.

"I'm here to talk to you about your son," I said.

"We've said all we're going to say to you about him."

"Oh, no. It's not that. I wanted you to know that he's safe."

She crossed her arms, huffing, "And how would *you* know?"

"It's complicated, but I'm sure you've been worried, and I wanted to put you at ease. Please, let me explain."

She hesitated, then stepped back. "Fine. Say what you came to say."

I felt it again, the same tight, coiled energy she carried the last time I was there. Fear disguised as control.

"I found Logan yesterday," I said.

"How?"

I'm a damn good private investigator, that's how.

"One of his friends tipped me off," I said.

She cocked her head to the side. "Which one?"

"What matters is, I convinced him to return with me to Cambria. He's staying at my place for now, while I investigate Audrey's murder."

A look of shock swept across her face, and then she swung the door open, motioning to the kitchen. "Come in."

We walked together down the hallway where I spotted Vaughn, who appeared to have been listening to our conversation.

The three of us sat down.

"Why is our son with you and not here, at home, where he belongs?" Tilly asked.

"Someone threatened him."

She pressed a hand to her chest, eyes wide.

"Threatened him, how?" she asked. "What kind of threat?"

"A direct one."

"From whom?"

"I don't know yet."

"That's not reassuring."

"I'm aware."

She stood, pacing the room and then flattened her hands on the counter. "Does Logan being threatened have anything to do with Audrey's murder?"

I nodded. "I believe she found some things someone didn't want her to find."

"What things?"

"It's connected to an old case," I said. "A young woman was visiting Cambria about twenty-five years ago, and she went missing. The case has never been solved."

Tilly and Vaughn exchanged worried glances, and Tilly shook her head. "You're being vague, talking in circles. I don't like it."

I needed to give her something but deciding what to offer proved harder than I thought.

"I spoke to your son yesterday, and I learned a great deal, things that have helped move this case forward," I said. "But right now, the fewer people who know where he is, or what he told me, the better."

"We're not *people*. We're his parents."

Vaughn wrapped his hand around a soda, looking at me with a displeased expression. "You're sitting here telling us our son has been threatened, and that he needs to stay with you right now, and you won't even give us any details or anything to go on? Why should we trust you?"

I faced him, getting the distinct feeling that something was off. While he wasn't being hostile or defensive, his tone was far different than it had been the first time we met.

I considered offering a breadcrumb, giving just enough information but not too much.

"Someone left Logan a note on his windshield several days

ago," I said. "It referenced Audrey. It told him to leave the past alone if he didn't want to end up like her."

Vaughn's grip tightened around the can. "And you believe the same person who killed Audrey is behind it?"

"I do."

"And this old case," he began, "this disappearance of a young woman … I suppose you think it's connected to Audrey and Logan and everything that's happening right now."

"I'd like to share more with you, but I can't. Not yet. I just need you to trust me and to know that I have your son's best interests at heart."

"*Trust*," he grunted. "You sound just like the police. You must be working with them."

"I am."

"Then why not let them handle it?"

"They are on their end," I said. "And I am on mine."

Silence stretched between us until Tilly broke it. "What do you want from us?"

"For now," I said, "I'm asking you not to tell anyone Logan has returned and is staying with me. Not friends. Not family. Not even neighbors."

"You're asking a mother to lie."

"I'm asking a mother to protect her son."

The comment seemed to strike a nerve.

"Fine," she said. "For now. But I want him to check in with me—daily."

"I will relay your message."

Vaughn stood, drinking down the last of his soda and then tossing the can at the trash can.

He missed.

"What assurances can you give us that our son is safe?" Vaughn asked.

"We have security, and I'm not talking about video surveillance. Actual security."

"Why?"

"My husband is involved in a line of work that requires it. All you need to know is that our house is the safest place Logan can be right now."

Tilly let out a frustrated sigh. "If he's staying with you, I'm guessing he's going to need some clothes."

"He does."

She moved past me toward the hallway, and Vaughn stepped closer, aiming a finger at me. "I want you to find who did this, and for it to all be over."

"I'm working on it."

Tilly returned with a duffel bag a couple of minutes later and shoved it into my hands.

"Tell him," she said, voice tight, "to call his parents."

"I will."

"And tell him that we love him."

I slung the bag over my shoulder and walked to the car feeling the conversation had gone as well as it could have gone.

As I sat in the driver's seat, I checked my phone.

A text from Whitlock waited.

We're heading to the cabin. They've started digging.

I responded:

I'll be there soon. I have much to tell you.

. . .

I turned the car toward home to pick up Giovanni who, having met Logan, was now just as invested in the case as the rest of us.

And I hoped today we'd find what we wanted most—*answers*.

26

Giovanni slid into the passenger seat of my car with a travel mug in one hand and his phone in the other. As we drove, we talked about the conversation I'd just had with Logan's parents, and he was pleased to hear the conversation went as well as it could have.

The forest seemed to swallow sound the closer we got to the cabin, the road narrowing until we reached a wide expanse, and what remained of the cabin came into view. The area looked nothing like it had the day before. The cabin was now demolished, and yellow tape marked a wide perimeter. Stakes and string were crisscrossed across the ground in careful squares, turning the clearing into a patchwork map.

The forensics team and a couple of members of the police department were working inside the grid. They wore gloves and kneepads as they crouched close to the earth, moving around with deliberate care.

Silas was easy to spot. He stood near the center of the grid, his clipboard tucked against his chest, directing the team with calm precision. They weren't shoveling. They were coaxing the ground open, inch by inch, using trowels and soft brushes to lift thin layers of soil without disturbing what might be hidden beneath.

"Silas is a lot more organized than I realized," Giovanni said.

"He knows how important it is to go over every inch of this place," I replied.

We got out of the car and walked toward the edge of the grid, careful not to step into any area that might disturb the ground. Foley spotted us first. He lifted a hand and came over. Whitlock was close behind, his tie already loosened, jacket slung over one shoulder.

"Morning," Foley said. "You picked a good time to show up. We're just getting into the second layer."

"Find anything yet?" I asked.

"A couple of pieces of vertebrae," Foley said. "That's it."

Whitlock smiled at Giovanni. "You bring coffee? It's going to be a long day."

Giovanni held up his mug. "I came prepared."

I filled them in on what had happened since we last spoke. Not every detail, just the pieces that mattered the most in this moment.

Logan.

The note.

The reason he ran.

And the reason he was now under our roof.

Foley and Whitlock listened, nodding along until I'd finished.

"That explains a lot," Foley said.

"Now we know why he ran," Whitlock added. "Can't say I blame the kid."

Foley glanced toward the grid. "Let's hope we find something today."

"Oh, we have something for you." I reached into my bag, pulled out the plastic bag Logan had given me the night before, and held it out. "When Logan got to Lost Prairie, he found this under a rock pile."

"How'd he know to look for it there?"

"Two things. First, not long before she died, Audrey made a comment about Lost Prairie being a place secrets go to hide. And second, they'd been there together before and built a stacked rock pile. When Logan arrived there, he noticed the shape of the pile had been changed. This was under it."

Foley took the bag, craning his head as he glanced inside to get a better assessment. "Looks like a piece of bone to me."

"I think it's a part of a pelvis," I said.

Foley nodded and turned, shouting for Silas to join us.

Silas came over, and Foley handed him the bag. Silas opened it and lifted the fragment, turning it in his hand. I told him how it had been found, and he said, "You're right. It does look like a pelvic fragment."

"Let's say it is, can you tell whether it's male or female?" Whitlock asked.

Silas pointed to the curve in the bone. "A female pelvis tends to be wider and rounder. Oval inlet. Lighter structure. This fits that profile."

"Could it be another piece of skeletal remains belonging to the same person?"

"Might be. I'll take it back for testing."

He placed it back into the bag with care and tucked it away. Then he gave the four of us a nod and headed back to the grid.

The hours passed, and we waited.

As the sun climbed higher, the team worked together, lifting soil, brushing dirt away, and marking each find with flags and notes. Giovanni and I took turns pacing the perimeter. As boredom set in, Whitlock told a story about a case he'd had two decades ago. The case had gone nowhere until an old key surfaced from the ground, a key that changed everything.

It gave me hope.

Late in the afternoon, Silas called us over, saying they'd found something.

We gathered near the grid as two small fragments were lifted free. More vertebrae from the looks of it.

Silas studied the finds and shook his head. "This doesn't make any sense."

"What doesn't make sense?" I asked.

"The vertebrae we've dug up today should have all been together, but they were not. I'm thinking ..." he said, rubbing his chin. "I'm thinking the site has been disturbed. I believe someone may have buried a body here at one time. Then they came back later and moved it. Except when they did, they missed a few pieces."

"Why move it?" Whitlock asked.

"Fear of the skeletal remains being found," I said. "Or guilt. Or both."

Silas nodded. "Either way, this is an unnatural scatter. The pattern doesn't fit."

Foley ran a hand along the back of his neck. "I guess I was hoping we'd find more, a lot more."

"We got enough," I said. "Enough to know someone was buried here."

"We'll start again in the morning," Foley said. "Fresh eyes. Fresh soil."

"And a fresh chance," Whitlock added.

The light began to fade, and the team covered the grid, the stakes they'd set remaining in place. Tomorrow, they'd widen the search, covering the area surrounding the one they searched today.

As we walked back toward the car, my frustration mounted.

I looked back at the cabin, at the strings stretched tight over the earth, at the place where secrets had been buried and almost never found. I believed Silas was right, and someone had come back here, someone with hopes to erase the misdeeds of the past.

27

I woke in the middle of the night to find myself inside the cabin. Not the ruined pile of splintered beams that had been scattered like broken bones after being torn down earlier that day. It was the way it had once stood, in the quiet weight of its history.

I leaned against one of the walls, my bare feet cold against the plank floor. Looking down, I was still dressed in a long, vintage black satin nightgown that skimmed the top of my feet.

As I took in where I was and why I was there, I heard something.

Not footsteps.

Not voices.

A slow, steady hum.

I turned to see a girl in the center of the room, brushing a broom across the floor with slow, deliberate strokes. She looked no older than seventeen, and her dark hair fell to her shoulders, straight and without style. Her simple, dated dress was stylish but faded at the hem. And when she moved, the light slid through her, as though she were there and not there at the same time.

"Hello," I said.

She gave me no acknowledgment.

I pushed away from the wall and took a step closer, the floor creaking beneath my feet.

Still, she didn't seem to notice me.

"Can you hear me?" I asked.

Nothing.

As she continued to hum, the tune became clearer and more defined, and I recognized the song. It was one my mother often played when I was a child. The girl stopped sweeping and lifted her head. Her eyes met mine, dark and knowing, as if she'd expected me and wasn't surprised.

"I'm Anne ... and you are?"

"Dreaming," I said.

"Sometimes dreams weave into reality. Did you know that?"

What I knew was that she wouldn't be around long.

In dreams like this one, they never were.

"I've been searching for you," I said.

"I know. You've been to the cabin twice this week."

"Why are you here?" I asked. "Or maybe I should say, why are you *still* here?"

She glanced around the cabin, her gaze lingering on the beam where her initials were carved. "We're here together."

"Who's here together? You and me?"

She moved a hand to her hip, nodding. "Who else would I be talking about?"

"Did you ever come to the cabin with anyone, someone you thought you could trust?"

She didn't answer. Instead, she stepped closer, the broom fading from her hands as she moved. The air grew colder with each step she took closer to me, as if the warmth of the room recoiled from her.

"Trust means different things to different people," she said.

"Were you murdered?"

"You're the private investigator. What do you think?"

"I think you were."

"Maybe you should trust your instincts, then. What else do they tell you?"

"The person who killed you also killed Audrey."

"Audrey was smarter than she realized, but she was also naïve."

"Did he or she, the one who murdered you, know Audrey found your locket?"

"He. She. Does it matter? I'm dead. If you don't want the same fate, maybe it shouldn't matter to you so much."

"Don't you want to be found, for your case to be solved?"

"I don't see why it matters anymore. Although ..."

The words trailed off, and she stood there, silent.

"What were you about to say?" I asked.

"It would be nice to leave this place."

"Did you ever consider you might be stuck here because your murder hasn't been solved?"

She shrugged. "Answers end things. Questions keep them alive."

"Is that your fear? You think if you're found, you won't be remembered anymore? Or that no one cared enough to keep looking until they found out what happened to you?"

"A bit of both, I suppose."

"I'll remember you, and I care."

"Yeah, you care about Audrey."

"And you."

She looked at me as if to say, "Prove it."

"I was placed where the land stayed still, where no one thought to look twice. I wasn't missing," she said. "I was hidden, until the truth refused to stay silent. What am I?"

"Bones. Your bones. I thought they would be here, but they are not."

She turned, pointing toward the doorway, then past it, into the darkness beyond. "They're not here. Not anymore."

"If not here, then where?"

"Follow the water, not the path, to the place where two are one."

"Water," I said. "What water?"

"It's time for you to go now."

"No, wait. I have more questions."

She went quiet, stepping backward, fading a little and then a little more until she was gone, and I was the only one left in the room. I squeezed my eyes shut, and when they opened, I woke with the echo of Anne's words still clinging to me:

Follow the water.

Not the path.

To the place where two are one.

28

A text message from Talia came through just after eight the next morning.

Any updates? I've heard a few things. I'm not sure what's true and what isn't.

I stared at the screen for a moment before replying.

A lot has happened since the last time we spoke. I'd rather talk in person.

Her response came without hesitation.

Can you come by?

.   .   .

I said yes, grabbed my coat, and headed out, driving the winding road to her home. Gabriel came to the door when I knocked, smiling as he said, "Georgiana, it's good to see you again. Talia told me you were stopping by. Come on in."

Today, the house smelled like coffee and toast, but there was no sign of Brianne.

"Is your wife here?" I asked.

"She's out running errands. I can see how long she's going to be if you'd like."

I swished a hand through the air. "Oh, no. It's fine. She doesn't need to be here."

We walked into the kitchen. The table was set with two mugs, one empty, the other full, and a plate of untouched pastries.

"Talia's in her room," he said. "I'll tell her you're here."

"Thank you."

He went upstairs and then returned, pouring me a cup of coffee before I had the chance to refuse it. Then he gestured toward the table. I sat, and he remained standing.

"How's Talia been since the last time I was here?"

"Worried and sad, just like we've all been."

"I can imagine."

"She's still not eating much or talking much."

Talia entered the room a moment later, her hair pulled into a loose braid, sweatshirt hanging off one shoulder. She crossed the room and wrapped her arms around me, a gesture I wasn't expecting.

Once she pulled back, she said, "I keep thinking we'll wake up, and we'll find out this has all been a big prank. And Audrey will walk through the door and laugh at us for falling for it."

"While we can't change what's happened, we can get justice for her and her family."

She searched my face. "You seem so confident that we will."

"I am."

She exhaled and sat across from me at the table. Gabriel joined us, folding his arms over the top of it.

"Can you tell us anything?" he asked.

"We're making progress," I said. "Before she died, Audrey found something connected to the past, an object someone wanted to stay buried."

Gabriel nodded, his expression solemn.

"I'm not surprised," Talia said. "Audrey picked up on everything, and she often noticed things other people missed.

"She also asked a lot of questions," Gabriel added. "She used to say her curiosity was her best and worst trait."

Talia reached for a pastry and popped it into her mouth. "What about Logan? Have you heard anything?"

I gave the question some thought, knowing I needed to choose my words with care. "I hear he's alive."

"How do you know?"

"He's been in contact with the police."

It was a lie, of course.

But I couldn't tell them the truth.

Not yet.

Talia's shoulders lowered. "So, he didn't just disappear."

"No."

"Is he okay?"

"He's distraught over what's happened," I said. "But he's doing his best to deal with it."

She nodded, accepting my answer without pressing me any further.

Gabriel studied me for a moment. "Did Logan tell the police why he took off like he did?"

"His girlfriend was murdered. Sometimes people do irrational things when they lose the person they love."

"That poor guy," Talia said. "The rumors going around town about him, they're unfair."

"I agree."

Gabriel cleared his throat. "Speaking of people behaving badly ..."

Talia glanced at her father. "*Dad.*"

"I haven't even said anything yet."

I looked at Talia, then at Gabriel. "What happened?"

"Logan's father has been by our house," he said. "Twice."

"When?"

"The first time was a couple days ago."

Before they knew their son was safe, and with me.

"What did he want?" I asked.

"He was upset, demanding to speak with Talia."

Talia drew a long breath. "I always thought he was a nice guy. But now, he kinda scares me."

"Why?" I asked.

"He's convinced Talia knows where Logan's at," Gabriel said. "He thinks she's been protecting him, for whatever reason."

"That's not true," she said. "I have no idea where he went."

"I know," Gabriel said. "I told him as much."

I thought back to my conversation with Tilly and Vaughn this morning. Vaughn had behaved in a way that was different from the first time we'd talked. Still, I didn't feel it was cause for concern.

"I'm surprised he came here," I said. "I've been told Logan had a closer relationship with Willow Robinson. I wonder why he wouldn't try and talk to her."

Or maybe he had.

"Have you met Willow's father?" Talia asked. "He's always

been super nice to me, but with others, he seems like the type of guy who would take a person out just because they looked at him the wrong way."

It was a fair assessment.

"What else did Vaughn say when he was here?" I asked.

"He didn't believe me, about Talia not knowing anything about where Logan was at," Gabriel said. "He accused me of lying. Said I was covering for my kid."

"Did he threaten you?" I asked.

"No," Gabriel said. "But he raised his voice, and there was something off about him. He's never acted that way toward me before."

"Maybe he was feeling a lot of pressure."

"Over what?"

"For starters, his son is missing," I said. "When the police first questioned him about it, he wasn't as truthful as he should have been."

It was a polite way of saying—he *lied*.

Talia looked at me. "Do you think Vaughn could have done something to Audrey?"

"I'm not sure."

"Does he know Logan is communicating with the police?"

"He knows his son is safe."

Once the words left my mouth, I realized I'd spat them out too fast.

And they'd caught Talia's attention.

"It was you," she said. "You talked to Vaughn and told him Logan was safe, didn't you?"

She may have thought Audrey was the curious one, but Talia was a little sleuth in the making herself.

"I talked to him, yes," I said.

Gabriel leaned forward. "Was that wise?"

"When I spoke to him, I had no idea he'd come here, trying

to find information about his son," I said. "Now that I do, it doesn't change anything."

"Why wouldn't it?"

"If Vaughn has nothing to hide, his mind is now at ease, and he won't come here again, looking for Logan. If he does have something to hide, Logan working with the police adds pressure on Vaughn."

Talia swallowed. "And if he's dangerous?"

"Then I expect he's about to make a big mistake," I said.

Gabriel studied me for a long moment. "You're certain Logan is protected."

"I am."

"It doesn't feel right, not being able to trust the people I've always trusted in this town," Talia said. "I feel like I'm judging everyone, whether they're innocent or not."

I placed a hand on her shoulder. "I'll have answers for you soon enough."

I stood, and Gabriel did the same.

"Whatever you need, let us know," he said. "We want justice for Audrey."

"I know," I said.

We said our goodbyes, and as I walked to the car, thinking about Vaughn, and giving him the location of his son.

If Vaughn was innocent, I had given him peace.

If he was not, a trap had now been set.

29

I had just pulled away from the curb when a call from Giovanni rang through the car speakers. When I answered, he said, "Good morning, *cara mia*. Where are you?"

"I just left Talia's house. Is everything okay?"

"Vaughn Lambert is at the gate, asking to see his son. What would you like me to do?"

I tightened my grip on the steering wheel. "Have Marco tell him that I'm on my way and I'll speak to him when I get there. What's his demeanor like?"

"Civil but uptight, from the information Marco gave me. How was your visit with Talia?"

"I spoke with her father, and he told me Vaughn has been by his house twice, demanding to speak with Talia. He accused her of knowing where Logan was and not telling them. This was before I spoke with him yesterday to let him know Logan was staying with us, of course."

"Do you consider him a suspect?"

"I didn't before. Now, I'm not so sure."

"Will you let him speak to his son?"

"Maybe. It might help me get a better read on him. His demeanor was a bit off when I last spoke to him."

"How can I be of help to you?"

"Your presence is all the help I need. Does Logan know his father's there?"

"I don't believe so. He's in the den, sketching."

"Will you let him know and ask him how he feels about speaking to his father?"

"I'll do it now."

We ended the call, and I sped up. When I turned onto our road, Marco's silhouette stood out near the gate. Vaughn's car idling in front of him.

A text message came through from Giovanni letting me know Logan had agreed to talk to his father.

I parked in front of the gate next to Vaughn, and I stepped out.

Vaughn did the same, walking over to me with his hands in his coat pockets, his posture rigid. His eyes flicked to the house, then back to me.

"Morning, Georgiana," he said.

"Morning. I hear you'd like to see Logan."

"I would."

"I don't think it's a good idea for you to see him yet."

It wasn't true, but I'd said it to gauge his reaction.

His expression tightened. "Why not?"

"It could compromise the investigation. No one is supposed to know he's here."

I heard footsteps coming from behind, and a moment later, Giovanni was at my side, introducing himself to Vaughn.

"I just want to see my son," Vaughn said. "I want to make sure he's all right."

"He's fine," I said. "It's just like I told you yesterday. He's safe, and he's protected."

Vaughn pointed at Marco. "By *him*?"

Marco met his gaze but said nothing.

"He's protected by Giovanni, and Marco, who's our security guard, and me," I said. "I just came from Gabriel Kinkaid's house. He told me you went to his house twice, trying to talk to Talia."

He nodded. "I was looking for my son."

"They said you were agitated, and when Gabriel refused to let you talk to Talia, you raised your voice."

"I did no such thing."

I moved a hand to my hip. "I'm just telling you what he told me."

"If you're not going to allow me to see my son, I will speak to the police about you keeping him here."

Giovanni and I exchanged glances.

"You can do whatever you like," I said. "Logan's eighteen. If he wants to be here, it's his decision."

"Please, just ... just let me see him."

I went quiet, hoping to give him the impression I was deliberating whether to give him what he wanted. "I'll let you speak to him, but we'd like to be in the room when you do."

Vaughn threw his hands in the air. "What you're asking is ridiculous. I get that you're looking out for him while you investigate Audrey's murder, but as the boy's father, I don't pose a threat, and you know it."

Except I *didn't* know it— not for certain.

"It's the only option I'm giving you," I said. "You can take it, or you can leave."

He hesitated, then nodded. "Fine."

"I need to speak to him first for a moment," I said. "Then you can."

Before he had the chance to respond, I turned toward the house, motioning for Marco to open the gate. We made our way to the house, and while Giovanni stood in the doorway with Vaughn, I looked for Logan. I found him at the kitchen table, eating a sandwich as Luka rested at his side.

"I wanted to make sure you're still all right with talking to your dad," I said.

"Yeah, it's fine. He's going to ask a lot of questions. He always does. What do you want me to tell him?"

"Everything, as much as you feel comfortable sharing."

He reached for a glass of water. "Why?"

Because I want to know if he acts suspicious.

Except I couldn't say that.

"It might be good to be honest with him about what's happened," I said. "Then maybe he'll be more comfortable with you staying here."

I stepped into the hallway, giving Giovanni a nod, and they joined us in the kitchen. As soon as Vaughn set his eyes on Logan, he rushed over, wrapping his arms around him.

"Son, I'm glad you're all right," he said. "We've been worried."

"I know," Logan said. "I'm sorry."

"I understand why Georgiana feels you need to be here, but you should come home. We can protect you."

Logan glanced at me, then back at his father, and he drew a breath. "I need to tell you something. Before Audrey died, she found something. A locket. It belonged to a girl who went missing many years ago."

Vaughn raised a brow. "What does this have to do with you?"

"Everything. Audrey was convinced the girl wasn't missing. She thought she was dead, that someone killed her. I think she was right."

Vaughn clenched his jaw a moment, then softened. "What made you both believe she was murdered?"

"There's this old cabin in the woods. It's where we found the locket. But I think Audrey found something else—a bone—a *human* bone."

"Why is this the first I'm hearing about it?" Vaughn asked.

"I just ... I wasn't sure, and then Audrey was murdered, and then someone left a note on my truck telling me to leave the past alone or I'd end up like her."

Vaughn froze, and I watched his face. The flicker of his eyes. The tightening of his mouth. The way his breath caught, then steadied.

Was it grief?

Fear for his son?

Or something else?

I couldn't be sure.

"I understand now why you left," Vaughn said. "But even after all you've told me, I'd like you to come home. Your mother and I can protect you."

"I'm safer here," Logan said.

"You're being ridiculous. You don't even know these people."

"I'm staying," Logan said.

Vaughn turned toward me, finger wagging. "This is *your* doing. You've put a bunch of nonsense into his head. You don't even know why Audrey was murdered yet. Might not have anything to do with this missing girl."

"It has everything to do with her," I said. "And as for your son, it's like I told you before. Staying is his decision."

"You're manipulating him, both of you."

"I'm looking out for him. Someone left a note on his truck. That doesn't concern you?"

"Of course it does. But it doesn't mean he needs to sit in this house until the investigation is over."

"He's staying," I said.

Vaughn leaned closer to me, and Giovanni stepped between us.

He didn't touch him, and he didn't speak.

But his silence sent a message.

"Stand aside," Vaughn said, his voice raised. "I'm getting my son out of here."

"Enough," Giovanni said. "You don't raise your voice in this house, and you don't make demands here."

"You have no right to tell me what to—"

"I have every right," Giovanni said.

Silence followed, thick and unyielding.

"Dad, I know what I'm doing," Logan said. "I need to stay."

Vaughn looked from Giovanni to Logan, then back again.

"This isn't over," Vaughn said.

"No," I said. "It isn't."

Vaughn jerked around and raced past us, heading for the front door.

Giovanni followed.

And I stood there, thoughts swirling around in my head.

One moment, I started to believe Vaughn was involved in Audrey's death somehow. The next, I wondered if he might be protecting someone—Tilly perhaps.

And that possibility unsettled me more than any other.

30

I arrived at the Ashfords' house around noon. The kitchen light was aglow as I pulled into the driveway, and it wasn't long before Rosemary peeked through the blinds and then met me at the front door.

"Good to see you," she said. "Come in."

I stepped inside, and Rosemary led me straight to the kitchen. She offered me a cup of coffee, which I accepted, and I took a seat beside her.

"How's the case going?" she asked. "Are you getting anywhere?"

"I am, and that's why I'm here," I said. "I have a few questions. You grew up around here, right?"

"Dustin and I both did."

"When I was here the other day, I told you about Anne, the young woman who went missing."

"I remember. What about her?"

"I think Audrey may have been investigating Anne's disappearance before she died," I said. "Anne would have been a little older than you when she went missing."

"Funny, I don't remember hearing anything about it."

"Did she ever ask you anything about your former class-mates at school?" I asked.

"Not about my classmates, no. But she did ask me if she could look through our yearbooks."

"When?"

Rosemary moved a hand to her hip. "Oh, let's see now, it would have been a couple of weeks before she died, if I remember right."

"Did she say why she wanted to look at them?"

"She said it was for history class. A final assignment about the school and its students through the years. She wasn't one to lie, so I didn't think to question it. Should I have?"

"Hard to say. How many yearbooks did she look at?"

"Seven. Dustin was three years ahead of me in school, so our Freshman and Senior yearbooks are the same."

"I'd like to see them, if you don't mind."

She nodded. "They're on a shelf in the coat closet. I'll get them."

Rosemary walked to the closet and opened it, pulling out a cardboard box. The lid came off with a faint scrape. Inside sat several yearbooks, their covers worn at the corners. She carried the box to the kitchen, and we spread the yearbooks across the table. Rosemary's name appeared in glitter pen on the inside cover of the first one, surrounded by dozens of faded signatures, some faded, others still holding up to the test of time.

I opened the first yearbook and began flipping through it. Rosemary leaned in beside me, pointing to faces, names, and the occasional scribbled note written in the margins.

"That was my friend Tara," she said, tapping on one of the photos. "She moved to Paso Robles after we graduated. Always thought we'd keep in touch, but for some reason we didn't."

I nodded but said nothing.

I didn't care about Tara or about strolling down memory lane.

I cared about patterns and clues, anything Audrey might have left behind that might be of use to me.

We worked through Rosemary's first yearbook and then the second. Nothing stood out. The third was more of the same. It was disappointing, but I wasn't ready to give up just yet. Audrey must have asked for the yearbooks for a reason, and I didn't believe it had anything to do with a school assignment.

Rosemary raised a finger. "Oh, I just thought of something I should have mentioned at the start. Audrey spent the most time going through Dustin's yearbooks, his senior year in particular."

The comment gave me hope.

"Which one is it?" I asked.

Rosemary slid one of the books to the side, grabbing the one beneath it and handing it to me. "This is the year we met."

I opened the book and began turning pages. When I came to the senior portraits, I noticed something strange—a black circle had been drawn around one of the portraits.

Not a neat pen mark.

A hard, deliberate ring drawn in thick marker.

I flipped through a few more pages and found another classmate had been circled.

Then another.

Then another.

I pointed out a few of the classmates that had been circled. "Before I make any assumptions, I just want to be sure you or your husband didn't draw these circles."

She leaned closer. "I did not. And as for Dustin, it doesn't seem like something he would do. It wasn't done in any of his other yearbooks."

Turning to the next page, my eyes landed on yet another circled photo, and Rosemary's hand flew to her mouth.

"That's ... that's Dustin." Her eyes darted to me, then back to the book. "Why would Audrey circle his photo?"

I wondered the same thing.

I also wondered if there was a connection, something linking everyone who had been circled.

My attention shifted to the next circled portrait, noting it was Talia's father, Gabriel Kinkaid. Not too far from it was another circle of Brianne, Gabriel's wife.

Two pages later, I saw that Vaughn Lambert's picture had also been circled, along with that of his wife, Tilly.

Logan's parents.

Then another, Aiden Robinson.

Willow's father.

It seemed they'd been chosen with purpose.

On the last page of the senior class portraits, two more faces had been circled, Jordan Ward and Wendy Ward. Twins. Their names meant nothing to me, but given they'd been circled, I imagined they soon would.

"I've spoken to everyone except the twins since your daughter died," I said. "What can you tell me about them?"

Rosemary glanced at their photos. "Ah, Wendy. She's one of my closest friends."

"She knew Audrey well, then?"

"I should say so. She's her godmother."

"And Jordan?"

"Haven't seen him much over the years. He lives on the other side of the world, in Sydney. Has an Australian wife and a few kids."

I thumbed through the rest of the book, finding nothing more of note, and then I snapped photos of every classmate Audrey—presumably—had circled.

Closing the book, I looked over at Rosemary. "When do you expect Dustin to be home?"

"He took a job out of town. He won't be back until tomorrow."

"The people who are circled, do they mean anything to you?"

"Yes and no."

"They must have been circled for a reason. What connection did those classmates have to you or your husband?"

"Since they were three years older than I was, we didn't run in the same circles," she said. "Dustin and I met when I was a freshman, but we didn't start dating until I was a senior. As to your question about them having a connection, there is one. There was a time when everyone circled had been good friends. Dustin told me they used to do everything together."

"What changed?"

She leaned against the wall, folding her arms. "It's just ... it was a long time ago, and I don't want to betray anyone's trust without talking to Dustin first."

"If telling me what you know helps me figure out what happened to your daughter, isn't it something you need to do, whether he would approve or not?"

She gave my comment some thought. "I suppose you're right. Here's what I remember. In high school, Vaughn and Tilly were dating, and as you know, they're now married. What most people don't know is, in their senior year, Tilly was stepping out on Vaughn with Aiden."

"Just so I'm clear, they were having sex, right?"

"Right. I knew nothing about it, of course, not until years later when I asked Dustin why the friend group had a falling out."

"What did he say?"

"He said they were all hanging out together at a bonfire one night. Tilly had too much to drink, and she started crying and just blurted it out, admitting she'd been having an affair."

"How did that go over?"

"Not well. He said everyone started arguing and picking sides. It got ugly. They may have disagreed on their feelings about the affair, but there was one thing they all agreed on. The secret needed to stay in the group. They made a promise not to speak of it to anyone else, not even their parents. And to my knowledge, they all kept that promise."

"Except Dustin told you," I said.

"I'd like to think we tell each other everything. And the secret was safe with me ... well, until now."

Affairs happened all the time, so I found it strange that they had made a pact to keep it between themselves.

"Is there any part of the story that you're leaving out?" I asked. "I don't understand why they'd make an actual pact to keep something like that between themselves. I'm even more surprised that it seemed to have worked."

"I haven't told you the worst part yet. Tilly didn't just admit the affair. She admitted she'd gotten pregnant but lost the baby before they could determine whether it was Aiden's or Vaughn's."

Now *that* was a secret worth keeping.

Even if the affair had caused tension within the friend group, two of them had lost a child, and that shared loss fostered empathy.

"What happened after that night?" I asked.

"They all went their separate ways. He said a few of them hung around here and there, but that it was never the same."

It was a lot to take in.

It felt like I was at a fork in the road, only this road had far more forks than one.

Turning to Rosemary, I said, "I think it's clear that Audrey was the one to circle those faces. When she gave you back the yearbooks, did she say anything about them? Did she seem nervous after that?"

Rosemary looked up as if searching her memories. "I remember thinking she was a lot more restless than usual in those final weeks, and she wasn't sleeping well. She kept checking her phone. I asked if she was okay, and she told me she was fine. I chalked it up to pre-college jitters."

I thought of Sadie's description of Audrey at the fast-food place.

The phone.

The tension.

Audrey was connected in some way to almost every person she had circled.

One of them had to be the killer.

"Did Audrey ever ask Dustin about his friend group?" I asked.

"Not to my knowledge."

"Were all the classmates Audrey circled present the night of the bonfire?"

"I'm not sure. Why don't I give Dustin a call, see if I can get him on the phone?"

She made the call, placing it on speaker when he answered. I filled him in on everything that had happened since I arrived at the house, and when I finished, I asked the question Rosemary had been unable to answer.

There was a long pause.

Too long.

"Dustin, are you there?" I asked.

"I, yeah. There was ... ahh, one other person there. I've been standing here trying to figure out the best way to tell you. The thing is, I didn't know."

"What didn't you know?"

"That Anne would be so central to your investigation. If I knew, I would have told you that Anne was with us that night."

Rosemary gasped, looking at me and mouthing, "I didn't know."

It was the biggest break in the case so far, and for a moment, I sat there, riveted, not knowing what to say next, and then it came to me.

"Who did Anne arrive with that night?"

"I don't know. She was just there. Given how explosive everything was that night, and the fact we were all drinking, a lot of it is a blur. I don't even remember her being introduced to any of us. It was maybe a week later when I read the article in the paper and found out she'd gone missing."

"Did you talk to any of your friends about it?"

"We got together once, right after we heard."

"Why?"

"Look, we may have been the last people to see Anne, and we didn't want the police to think one of us had anything to do with it. We didn't."

"Let me guess, the pact you all made was more about Anne and less about Tilly?"

"I ... yes. I'm sorry. I'm so sorry."

Rosemary, who appeared to be in shock, looked at me and said, "If you don't mind, I believe I need to have a talk with my husband in private."

"Not at all," I said, standing to leave. "If you think of anything else, please let me know."

I walked to my car with one thing on my mind—the ring of names, all connected by a shared past.

All connected to Cambria.

All connected, now, to Anne Fontaine.

31

Wendy Ward lived on the quiet side of Cambria, in a small cottage tucked between two larger homes that looked like they'd been renovated one too many times. Hers hadn't been. The paint was a soft teal that had started to fade, the kind of color chosen by someone who liked it because it made them happy, not because it was on trend.

I parked at the curb and sat for a moment, rereading the address Rosemary had messaged me after I left her house.

Wendy answered the door as soon as I knocked, and I assumed Rosemary had given her a heads-up that I was coming.

She was tall and thin, with silver-blond hair that fell to her shoulders. Oversized black glasses sat low on her nose, and she wore a cardigan several sizes too big over a black dress with symbols of the sun and the moon all over it.

"Wendy Ward?" I asked.

She nodded. "That's me."

"I'm Georgiana Germaine. I'm investigating Audrey Ashford's murder."

"Yes," she said. "I was told you'd be stopping by."

"If it's a good time, I have a few questions."

She stepped aside, and I walked in, noticing a plethora of plants crowding every counter and every windowsill, some healthy, others clinging to life.

"I've been meaning to catch up with Rosemary about the investigation for a few days now," she said. "We've been playing phone tag, haven't seemed to find a time that works for us both. Maybe you can fill me in on what's going on."

"I'll do my best."

We moved into the living room, and she gestured toward the couch, then sat in an armchair opposite me, curling one leg beneath the other.

"I've been thinking a lot about Audrey since she died," she said. "She came to see me, not too long before she … she …"

Wendy turned, staring out the window as she wiped the tears from her cheeks.

"What did the two of you talk about?" I asked.

"She had a lot of questions. At the time, I thought we were having a casual, innocent conversation. Now, I'm not sure what to think."

"What were her questions?"

"Audrey wanted to know about my last year of high school and the group of friends I hung out with back then. She said it was for a history assignment."

"She went through Rosemary's and Dustin's yearbooks, and she told them the same thing. But I don't believe there ever was a history assignment. I think she was trying to find out what happened to Anne Fontaine. Did she ask you about her?"

"I mean, you don't think she was digging into the past and someone put a stop to it, do you?"

"That is exactly what I think."

Wendy shook her head, mumbling, "I had no idea, or I wouldn't have said anything. The last time I saw Audrey, she asked me if I'd ever met Anne. I said yes, I'd met her once. I didn't think admitting it now, after all these years, was a big deal. The case is cold. No one is looking into it anymore."

"They weren't before, but they are now. What else did the two of you talk about?"

Wendy leaned back, thinking. "She asked me to tell her what I knew about Anne, which was minimal."

"What did you say?"

"I told her I was with my girlfriends one night, and we'd stopped at a store to get some snacks before we met the boys at the beach to have a bonfire. They'd gone to the liquor store to try and talk someone into buying them some beer."

"How did Anne fit into the equation?"

"She was in the store, standing by the freezer, looking lost. She asked the clerk a question about directions, then she turned and she saw us."

"What did she say?"

"She was in town visiting her aunt, and she admitted she didn't know anyone around her age. I thought it would be a good idea to invite her to the bonfire, so I asked, and she accepted."

"How did Anne seem that night?"

"Excited to hang out with us, and grateful that we'd invited her along. She was nice and funny. I liked her. A couple of days later, rumors started going around town that Anne was missing. I guess she never made it back to her aunt's house after the bonfire."

"Which means you all were the last ones to see her."

Wendy nodded. "When the paper ran an article about her disappearance, my stomach dropped. I wanted to believe she was fine, that what we were hearing were rumors or that she'd been found. But she hadn't been."

"And you didn't go to the police."

"No," she said. "None of us did."

"Why not?"

"We were young and stupid, and we knew we were the last ones to see her. We weren't just worried about that. We were all drunk that night. I think we all were, at least. When we got together to talk about Anne, we were talking about what we remembered and about how the night ended, but no one had a specific recollection. We each had either no recollection or vague ones. Since none of us had anything to do with what happened to her, so we decided it was better not to talk to the police."

"You're assuming no one in your friend group had anything to do with what happened to Anne. In truth, one of them could be lying, keeping a secret for all these years."

"Maybe you're right, but we figured once the police started asking questions, they wouldn't stop. There was a lot going on in our friend group at the time, things we didn't want to be dragged into the open."

"Secrets like the relationship between Tilly and Aiden."

"How do you know about it?"

"It doesn't matter, does it?"

She let out a heavy sigh and closed her eyes. When she opened them again, she said, "We convinced ourselves that maybe Anne didn't have a happy home life, and when she got to Cambria to visit her aunt, she'd taken the opportunity to run away."

"From what I can tell, she had a good home life, and what you all did was create a lie to ease your guilt. You had to know staying silent instead of going to the police was wrong."

"I know. I've had years to think about it, believe me."

"Did you tell Audrey about the affair between Tilly and Aiden?"

"I didn't. It's not my story to tell."

It seemed she was being straight with me, but the longer we spoke, the more I wondered if there were other secrets she was hiding.

"You may not have gone into details about that night, but having grown up here, in such a small town, Audrey was connected to just about everyone in your former friend group," I said.

"Yeah, I guess when I talked to her, I didn't think it through. I didn't know that Anne was in any way connected to Audrey's murder. If I had, I would have said something sooner. I swear."

"You seem to be telling the truth," I said.

Her shoulders slumped in relief, but the guilt was still written all over her face.

"Now I'm thinking," she said, "if I had kept my mouth shut, maybe Audrey would still be alive."

"Or maybe she would have found out another way to get to the truth," I said. "Curiosity has a way of pushing through cracks."

We sat in silence for a time, and then I said, "At the bonfire, did Anne talk to any one person more than the others? One of the boys, perhaps?"

"To be honest, once the truth about Tilly and Aiden came out, my focus was on Tilly. Everyone was yelling at each other, and there she was, mourning the loss of a child. No one seemed to be focusing on that or caring about what she was going through, except for me."

I leaned forward, looking Wendy in the eye. "My opinion is that someone in your group is responsible for Anne's disappearance, what I believe was her murder, and Audrey's as well. I just haven't been able to prove it yet."

I stood, the puzzle pieces shifting in my mind as I realized I was homing in on the killer. "Thank you for being honest with me."

Wendy nodded. "Are you close to figuring out the person responsible for Audrey's death?"

"I'm a lot closer today than I was yesterday," I said.

She wiped away a few more tears, reaching for a tissue as she said, "That's something, I guess."

I walked out the door, and as it closed behind me, I stared out at the quiet street, thinking about a night at the beach, a girl who'd trusted the wrong people, and a former circle of friends who were still bonded in silence ... until now.

32

I'd driven to the end of Wendy's street when my phone buzzed against the console. I glanced at the screen, expecting a message from Foley or Whitlock.

Instead, I saw Vaughn Lambert's name.

I pulled over, letting the engine idle while I read the text.

I spoke with Tilly after I left your house, and we need to talk to you. Could you come by the house when you get a chance?

I stared at the message a moment longer, weighing the timing. Given it was almost six o'clock, I'd planned to call it a day, giving myself some time to take in everything I'd learned today and set up my plans for tomorrow. I also didn't like the way the last conversation had gone with Vaughn, and I wasn't interested in going for round two. Earlier, he'd stood in my kitchen demanding his son come home. Now he wanted my time, my attention, and, I assumed, my information.

Had they been alerted to the fact that I knew about the night of the bonfire and the secrets they'd been keeping all these years?

I needed to know.

I'm nearby, I typed back. *I can stop by.*

He responded right away.

Thank you. We'll be here.

I put the car back into gear and headed toward their neighborhood, the ocean fog rolling in low and slow as day turned to night. Tilly opened the door when I arrived, and her demeanor felt a lot different than the last time I'd seen her, less rigid and not wound as tight. Her hair was pulled back, her sleeves rolled to her elbows. She offered me a faint smile as she invited me in.

"We appreciate you coming over so soon," she said.

Who was this woman?

And what had they done with Tilly?

Vaughn stood in the kitchen, leaning against the counter with his arms crossed. He straightened when he saw me, his expression cautious but controlled.

"I didn't think we'd be seeing each other again so soon," he said.

"Neither did I," I replied. "What's on your mind?"

"Before we get to that, I want to apologize about my

behavior this morning," he said. "I now see all that you're doing for our son. It means a lot to us."

First Tilly.

Now Vaughn.

It was like I'd stepped into an episode of *The Twilight Zone*.

Tilly nodded, then gestured toward the table. "Please. Sit."

Vaughn cleared his throat. "After I saw you this morning, I came home and told Tilly everything Logan had said about the locket, the cabin, and the missing girl."

Tilly nodded. "Vaughn told me that no one ever mentioned her name. But when he described her—where she disappeared, the timing, the cabin—it felt familiar. Too familiar. And I started thinking."

"We were wondering if the locket Audrey found belonged to a young woman named Anne," he said.

My pulse quickened, though I tried to remain unfazed by his comment.

"Yes, the locket belonged to Anne," I said.

Outside, a gull cried, the sound sharp against the stillness of the room.

"We never imagined," Tilly said. "Not once did we consider her name would come up again after all this time. Or that she could be tied to what happened to Audrey."

"And now?" I asked.

"Now we want to help," Vaughn said.

Of course they did.

Because they were also tied to Anne and to Audrey, which landed them in a prime position on my suspect list. I couldn't decide whether they were being straight with me or working together to butter me up. If it was the latter, they would soon find it was a waste of time.

Vaughn cocked his head to the side, looking at me like he

knew what I was thinking. "We swear to you, we had nothing to do with Anne's disappearance or Audrey's murder."

"I hear you," I said. "But I need more than assurances."

Tilly nodded. "We understand. How can we give them to you?"

"Tell me about the bonfire," I said. "Start from the beginning. What you remember. What you saw. Who left first. Who stayed the longest. Everything."

Vaughn and Tilly exchanged a tense glance.

"How do you know about the bonfire?" Tilly asked.

"I have my ways."

Tilly crossed one leg over the other. "It was supposed to be a great night. And then it all went wrong."

"Tell me how Anne fits into it all."

"A few of us met her at the convenience store, and Wendy, who always wants to know everything about everyone she meets, learned Anne was in Cambria visiting her aunt, and she invited Anne to join us."

"She seemed nice," Vaughn added. "A bit on the quiet side from what I recall, but she was kind to everyone."

"Did she have anything to drink? And by drink, I mean alcohol."

"If she did, I didn't notice," Tilly said. "While I was there, she stayed close to Wendy."

"And you two?" I asked. "What were you doing?"

Vaughn looked down at the floor. "Arguing."

Tilly's jaw tightened, and they both went quiet.

"I know about the affair, and the baby," I said. "You just told me it was supposed to be a great night, but from what I heard, you were suffering even before you got there. I can't imagine it would have been a great night for you either way."

"I'd hoped having a bit to drink would help drown out my

emotions. It did the opposite. I had too much to drink, and before I knew it, I'd confessed everything."

"What happened next?"

"Everything blew up," Vaughn said. "Everyone was weighing in with their opinions and judgments. It was too much for me to handle, so I left."

"When?"

"Earlier than most, I guess."

"Did you drive?"

He shook his head. "I walked."

I turned toward Tilly. "What did you do?"

"I went after him. I thought if I could talk to him, maybe we could salvage our relationship."

"Are you saying you left together?" I asked.

"Not together," Vaughn said. "I left first. Then she chased after me."

"Did either of you see Anne again after that?"

"No," Tilly said.

"Did you see who she was with when you left?"

They shook their heads in unison, and Tilly said, "I was so caught up in what had happened that night, I didn't give Anne another thought—not until we found out she was missing."

"And that's when the group met again," I said.

"Yes," Vaughn said. "We were all still angry, but when we realized we might have been the last people to see her, we set aside our grievances so we could figure out what to do next."

"And you all decided to make a pact."

"I'm ashamed to say we did," Tilly said. "We agreed that if any of us were interviewed by the police, we'd all say we were together that night, but we wouldn't mention the fact that Anne was with us."

"We were afraid," Vaughn said. "Afraid if she wasn't found, one of us could be blamed for something we didn't do."

"And no one questioned that decision later?" I asked.

Tilly shook her head. "We convinced ourselves whatever happened to Anne had nothing to do with us."

I sat back, taking in their story.

It fit, but almost in a way I found too neat.

"Now we see how wrong we were," Vaughn said. "If Audrey was digging into this, and if someone killed her to keep the past from coming out, I wish we would have spoken up back then."

It was a comment I kept hearing over and over as I'd started speaking to all those at the bonfire that night.

"Do you believe one of your friends could be responsible for what happened to Anne and for Audrey's murder?" I asked.

Tilly looked at the floor, and Vaughn hesitated.

"I can't say it's impossible," Vaughn said. "But no. I don't think anyone in our group had anything to do with what happened to either one of those women."

It occurred to me that Vaughn or Tilly or both may have searched their son's room before he took off or after. They could have stumbled upon the hidden notebook, seen the rendering of the locket. If so, Vaughn or Tilly might be the killer, or one could be covering for the other. They were two theories I wasn't ready to lay to rest.

"What about you two?" I asked. "You say you're innocent, but you have yet to convince me."

"We're cooperating, telling you everything we know," Tilly said.

"You are now, and I'm willing to bet it's because the truth is starting to come out."

"We're owning up to the mistakes of our past to protect our son."

"And because it's the right thing to do," Vaughn added.

Was it because it was the right thing, though?

Or was it out of necessity and the need to appear innocent?

"Is there anything else I need to know, anything you haven't told me already?" I asked.

Vaughn met my gaze, and they both said no.

"We want this solved," Tilly said. "For Anne. For Audrey. For everyone who needs answers."

"I do too," I said. "And in that vein, I have a few more questions."

33

I leaned back and asked the question that had been circling my mind since I arrived. "How did the two of you end up getting back together?"

Tilly glanced at Vaughn, and for the first time since I'd sat down with them, something unguarded passed between them.

Not tension.

Not strategy.

Appreciation for one another.

"We didn't," Vaughn said. "Not right away."

Tilly nodded. "We were apart for six months."

"Six months," I repeated.

"I left town for a bit after the breakup," Vaughn said. "Stayed with my older brother. I needed distance. Every time I thought about Tilly, I thought about everything that happened and everything I'd lost."

"Did either one of you ever consider reaching out to each other during that time?" I asked.

Tilly folded her hands in her lap. "I'd done enough damage. If we were going to get back together, I wanted it to be on his terms, and not by me trying to force it."

"How did it happen?"

Tilly smiled as if recalling the memory. "At a gas station, of all places."

Vaughn nodded. "I was filling up my truck. I looked up, and she was standing on the other side of the pump. When our eyes met, she took one look at me and broke down."

Tilly shook her head. "I tried to hold it together, but seeing him like that, after all we'd been through, it broke something open in me."

"As angry as I was," Vaughn said, "I could still see how much pain she was in. I walked over and hugged her."

"And that was enough to start things again?"

"Not right away," Tilly said. "We took it slow. Coffee. Walks. Talking through everything."

"The love was still there," Vaughn said. "It just needed time to breathe so it could rebuild again."

They sat closer now, their shoulders touching, and it was easy to see that whatever they had rebuilt still held strong today.

"Thank you for sharing your story with me," I said. "Now I'd like to switch topics and talk to you about the friend group."

"The *former* friend group," Vaughn said. "But yeah, I figured you would."

"All right, let's start with Aiden."

His jaw tightened. "Even before the affair, there was something off about him."

"Off how?"

"He sat back, studied people ... or *scrutinized* them might be a better word. Some of our other friends thought he was great, but I never trusted him."

"What about Gabriel?"

Vaughn snorted a laugh. "Gabriel was the opposite. Always

joking. Always pulling pranks. If there was tension in the room, he could always cut through it with humor."

"He liked being liked," Tilly said. "Still does, I imagine."

"And his wife, Brianne?"

"She was the type of person who always remembered everyone's birthdays and worried about them getting home safe," he said.

His assessment seemed spot on. Every time I spoke to Brianne it was easy to see how concerned she was about Talia.

"And Dustin, Audrey's father?"

"That man would give you the shirt off his back," Vaughn said. "And if you told him something in confidence, it stayed with him. He's one of the best men I've ever known."

"And last, the twins, Jordan and Wendy."

"Jordan and Wendy were inseparable," Tilly said. "Always finishing each other's sentences. It was funny. They're both good people."

"Wendy talked," Vaughn said. "A lot."

"But her heart was always in the right place," Tilly added. "She never meant any harm."

Up to now, the conversation had been light.

That was about to change.

"Hypothetical question," I said. "If you had to choose one person in your friend group as the person responsible for Anne's disappearance and Audrey's murder, who would it be?"

Vaughn answered without pause. "Aiden."

"Why?"

"Because of what I said about him before. Never thought the guy could be trusted."

I turned to Tilly.

She was silent for a long moment, and then she said, "I don't feel comfortable naming any of them. At one point, they were all my friends."

"But if you had to choose," I pressed.

"I don't know, Brianne, I guess."

Vaughn looked at her, surprised. "Why Brianne?"

"She's just, I don't know, perfect," Tilly said. "Or that's what she wants people to believe, anyway. People who never crack scare me. They know how to hide things, and from my experience with people like that, most of the time they are."

Two names.

Two motives.

No proof.

I stood, slipping my coat over my arms as I reached for my bag.

"Thank you," I said. "This helps more than you realize."

As I walked toward the door, one thought refused to let go.

I was getting close to finding a killer.

34

I woke with the feeling that time was no longer on my side. Not because the case had gone cold, but because it was heating up, and when that happened, people either talked or panicked. Sometimes both. As I began getting ready for the day, a text message came through from Silas. The scarf yielded no DNA evidence, but the hair caught in Anne's locket was confirmed to be hers.

Today, I was intent on speaking with Aiden, to see what he had to say about the night of the bonfire.

His house sat farther inland than most, tucked behind a stand of eucalyptus trees that peeled and shed like they were trying to escape their own skins. The place suited him. It was private and defensive, perhaps even a little hostile.

I knocked, and when no one came to the door, I knocked again.

Still nothing.

I was about to head back to my car, when the door opened.

Aiden stood there with the same expression he'd had the last time I saw him, like he was annoyed that I existed. Today, he was dressed in a pair of stained jeans and a white tank top, even though it was mid-winter.

"You again," he said. "What is it now?"

"I need to ask you about the bonfire," I said. "And about Anne Fontaine."

He snorted, stepping back. "Someone's been getting people to talk."

"What can I say? I am good at my job."

"Looks like everyone's decided to dredge up ancient history. Guess you better come in then."

I stepped inside, taking in a faint smell of sawdust. There were no personal touches around the house, no warmth. It reminded me of a home someone lived in but never loved.

He motioned toward a chair but didn't sit himself, choosing instead to lean against the counter with his arms crossed.

"Who's been running their mouth?" He raised a finger. "Wait, lemme guess. Was it Wendy?"

"Among others."

"What others?"

I hesitated, refusing to answer.

"Look," he said. "If you want me to talk, you need to do a little talking yourself."

"Fine. I've spoken with several people in your old friend circle. The most recent being Vaughn and Tilly."

He rolled his eyes. "Figures. Let me guess. They painted me as the villain of the group."

"They painted you as untrustworthy."

He laughed. "That all? How generous. Bet they didn't tell you I dated Tilly first."

No, they did not.

"The affair makes a lot more sense to me now," I said.

"Back then, when we were dating, I thought everything was

fine between us. Next thing I know, she's dropping me for that jerkoff."

"Why?"

"Vaughn's safe and predictable, like a spud with no toppings. And, honey, I have plenty of toppings to go around."

Gross.

"How did the affair happen?" I asked.

He raised a brow. "How about we stop calling it an affair, like we were married or something, and call it what it was—sex."

"Fine, how did you two end up having sex?"

"I'm better in the sack than him, for starters. She came to me. Said something about being in love with Vaughn but still missing me. I gave her the best of both worlds. For one night, anyway. She felt so guilty over it, she wouldn't agree to do it again. Then she got pregnant and lost the kid, as I'm sure you know, since you seem to know everything else. You wanna know what I think?"

"I do."

"I think she still has feelings for me, even now. Some people don't forget their biggest mistake, if you know what I mean."

His comment told me everything I needed to know about how he viewed himself.

"Let's talk about Anne," I said. "What do you remember about meeting her?"

He shrugged. "The missing girl? She was polite. Flirty. Talked to all of us."

"All of you," I repeated.

"Well, from what I can remember, she spent a lot of time with Vaughn and Gabriel," he said.

Interesting.

"You're sure it was those two?"

"As sure as I can be after a few beers," he said. "But don't get the wrong idea. I could hold my liquor back then. Still can."

"I'm sure," I said.

"Anne laughed a lot," he continued. "Loud and pitchy. Seemed to like attention. Didn't strike me as shy."

Aiden's description of her didn't match Wendy's.

Or Rosemary's.

"Everything was going fine that night, and then Tilly couldn't keep her trap shut," he said. "Ruined the entire evening. Everything went to hell after that."

"What did you do?"

"Sat back, watching everyone tear into each other. I did what I could to stay out of it. Someone had to keep things from getting worse."

That was an interesting way to think of it.

"Would you say you stayed the longest?" I asked.

"Yeah, I'd say. Oh, and Anne was still there when Vaughn left the first time."

"The *first* time?"

"He'd stormed off after Tilly's confession because he couldn't handle it. Tilly went after him. He came back later. Just him though, not Tilly."

Vaughn and Tilly hadn't mentioned that fact to me.

And Tilly had said they didn't return.

Was she lying?

Or hadn't she known that Vaughn went back?

"When did Vaughn return to the bonfire?" I asked.

"Later. After things had settled some. He'd broken things off with Tilly, and he wanted to keep drinking."

"And you're sure Anne was still there then?"

"I think so. At some point, she left."

"Alone?"

He shook his head. "I don't think so. I don't remember."

"So, you remember her talking to Vaughn and Gabriel, but not who she left with at the end of the night."

"That's what I just said."

"It seems a little convenient," I said.

His posture stiffened. "You accusing me of something?"

"I'm saying it seems to me like you're steering the story in the direction you want it to go."

"Or maybe I'm the only one who's being honest with you."

"About what?"

"That Anne wasn't some innocent little lamb the papers portrayed her to be back then," he said.

There it was, at last.

The subtle shift.

Blame the victim.

Blur the edges.

Make her seem less like a victim and more like a person who deserved what happened to her.

"Did you offer Anne a ride?" I asked.

"No."

"Did Gabriel?"

"I don't know."

"Did Vaughn?"

He hesitated.

"Maybe," he said. "Wouldn't surprise me."

"Why?"

"My guess? After what went down, he needed to feel wanted that night."

"One last thing," I said. "How did you feel about Gabriel back then?"

He raised a brow. "He was an insecure little clown."

"Did you trust him?"

Aiden laughed. "I never trust anyone who needs to be liked as much as he did."

I nodded. "That's all I need."

"Good, you can see yourself out."

As I walked back to my car, the pieces shifted again.

Aiden was shaping the truth until it fit the version of himself he wanted to believe. He remembered details when they benefited him. Lost them when they didn't.

But one thing stood out.

Anne didn't vanish into the night.

She stayed after the argument between Tilly and Vaughn.

She stayed after Vaughn left the first time.

She stayed after the group fractured.

And she must have left with someone.

Someone who made people feel safe, even when they weren't.

35

Brianne looked surprised when she answered the door, seeing me standing on the front porch without warning, unlike our previous visit.

"Oh. Georgiana," she said. "I didn't expect ... come in."

The house was quiet today. No television. No radio. Just the faint tick of a clock somewhere down the hall.

"Is Gabriel home?" I asked.

"No," she said. "He took the car into town. Talia's out too."

We walked into the kitchen, where a kettle sat cooling on the stove. Two mugs were already out, untouched. She motioned for me to sit, then took the chair across from me, folding her hands together like she was bracing herself for the reason for my visit.

"I'm guessing you didn't come by just to check in," she said.

"No," I said. "I didn't. I want to share a few more details about the case and the things that have come to light since I saw you last."

She raised a brow. "Okay."

"I know Anne Fontaine was at a bonfire with you and several of your friends right before she went missing. I also know you all agreed not to give the police that information after she disappeared."

Brianne sighed and said, "You're right. Aiden convinced us not to tell the police. He thought they'd try to blame one of us for her disappearance. It was a long time ago, though, and I guess I just don't understand what Anne has to do with the reason why you're here."

"Audrey found Anne's locket," I continued. "And I believe that's what led to her murder."

"How so?"

"After she found it, she started asking questions, trying to figure out what had happened to her. Ask me, the person responsible for her murder knew Audrey was looking into Anne's disappearance."

"No one knows what happened to Anne. I don't see why someone would kill Audrey over an idle curiosity for a missing woman. If the police couldn't figure out what happened to her, Audrey wouldn't have been able to either, not after all this time."

"The police lacked evidence we now have. They never knew your friends were with her right before she went missing. Audrey knew the truth."

"Who told her?"

I thought about whether I should tell her or not, but at this point, I thought it all deserved to be out in the open.

"Wendy," I said.

"I am surprised Wendy kept it to herself for all this time. I always knew not telling the police was the wrong decision. I just didn't want to be the only one who did and then have them question everyone else, and have them contradict my story. Once one person talks, everything comes out. And that night, it wasn't just about Anne. There were other things happening. Things people wanted to forget."

"Secrets," I said.

"Yes."

She fidgeted with the collar on her shirt, straightening it even though it was already straight.

Her nerves were getting the better of her.

That much was obvious.

Maybe she'd realized that even after all this time, they could all be in trouble for withholding information.

Or maybe she was nervous for a different reason.

"Tell me what you remember about the bonfire," I said.

She leaned back, drumming her fingers over the table. "I remember the fire, the sound of the waves, and everyone laughing at first. Gabriel being Gabriel, telling jokes, keeping things light."

"And Anne? What did you think of her?"

"She seemed a little overwhelmed with us at first, maybe. But she was nice and polite."

"That's not how Aiden described her," I said.

Her brow furrowed. "What did he say?"

"He said Anne was flirty, and that she talked most to Gabriel and Vaughn that night."

Brianne frowned. "I don't remember that. I remember her laughing. I'm embarrassed to admit I threw up a few times, so I wasn't around for everything. I spent part of the night away from everyone, sitting on the sand, trying not to pass out."

"When was that?" I asked.

"After Tilly told everyone about the affair. Everything got loud and emotional, and I couldn't handle it."

"Do you remember Anne talking with Vaughn?"

Brianne hesitated.

"I do," she said. "But it's blurry. I remember them laughing together."

"When?"

"I think it was later on, after Vaughn came back."

Vaughn returning had now been confirmed by Brianne as well as Aiden, and I assumed the two of them hadn't been in contact to get their stories straight.

"Did you see Anne leave?" I asked.

Brianne shook her head. "I left before she did."

"With whom?" I asked.

"I'd told my mom we were having a bonfire that night. She knew how crazy those nights could get. She always told me I wouldn't get in trouble for anything as long as I told her the truth, so at some point, she picked me up."

Maybe Brianne's mother could fill in the gaps of what happened that night.

"Does your mother still live in the area?" I asked.

She shook her head. "She died last year."

"I'm sorry."

"It's all right. We spent a lot of time together during the last year of her life. Made a lot of good memories."

She went quiet, staring out the window as if reminiscing about old times.

"I don't believe Audrey was killed by a stranger," I said. "I believe she told the wrong person about what she'd found out, someone she thought she could trust."

Brianne stared at the table, her shoulders slumping. "I keep thinking, if I'd gone to the police back then, maybe none of this would've happened."

"Or maybe it would've happened sooner," I said. "We can't know that for sure."

She nodded.

"I was hoping to talk to Talia," I said. "Do you know when she'll be back?"

"She's down at the creek. Been going there a lot the past few days. Says it helps to clear her head. She says she feels closer to

Audrey when she's there. I'll tell her you stopped by, and I'll have her reach out to you."

I said goodbye and stepped outside, the air feeling colder than when I arrived. I drove down the road and parked off to the side, hiding my car from view. Then I got out, hoping to find Talia.

I walked toward the creek feeling I was close to finding the truth, to discovering not just what happened to Audrey, but to Anne.

It was as if the truth was waiting to be discovered, just out of sight.

36

It took a lot longer than I'd hoped, but I found Talia at the creek, sitting on a fallen log with her boots planted in the damp soil, her elbows resting on her knees as she stared at the slow-moving water. The creek whispered as it wound its way through the trees, the sound steady and soft, making me see why she was so fond of this place.

She looked up when she heard me approach, and relief crossed her face.

"Hi," she said. "I didn't know you were coming over today."

"I just spoke with your mom. She told me you were out here."

"I come here when all the noise in my head gets too loud."

I knew the feeling.

"I wanted to fill you in on some of the things that have happened since we last spoke," I said. "Some of it won't be easy to hear."

She straightened, brushing her hands over her jeans. "It's okay. Whatever it is, I want to know."

I sat on the log beside her, and for a moment, we both watched the water slide past, leaves drifting along its surface.

"I need to tell you about Anne Fontaine. She was a girl who went missing a long time ago."

"Was she ever found?"

"She wasn't. I believe Audrey found the locket at the cabin. Once she realized it belonged to Anne, she learned a woman by that name had gone missing and began asking questions. At first, they were limited. As she uncovered more about Anne's disappearance, those questions grew."

I went on to tell her about the bones, the bonfire, the pact the group made after Anne disappeared, and everyone who was involved. I also explained my theory that as Audrey started piecing it all together, her curiosity may have turned to obsession.

Talia listened without interrupting, her hands clenched together in her lap.

"I believe someone knows what happened to Anne and that Audrey was trying to figure out who," I said. "The harder she dug into it, the more they felt threatened until they decided something had to be done so the truth would stay buried."

"What are you saying?"

"I think Anne left with someone at the bonfire that night, and then something happened, and that's why she went missing. Except I don't think she's missing. I believe she's dead and that the person responsible for her death is either responsible for Audrey's death too or connected to it in some way."

"If the last people to see Anne were at the bonfire, you're saying you think … no. That can't be true. My parents were there, and it isn't either of them. They loved Audrey. She was family."

"I don't doubt that," I said. "But love doesn't erase fear. And it doesn't cancel out the instinct to protect yourself when a secret pushes its way to the surface."

Talia wrapped her arms around herself. "You're wrong. You have to be. Everyone who was there, they're all good people."

"I wish I were."

Her eyes filled with tears, and she turned away, staring at the water again. "I don't know how to take what you just said. It feels like the ground just shifted under me."

"I know, and I'm sorry for all you're going through right now."

She wiped at her cheek. "I think I want to go home. Can you walk me back? I don't want to be alone right now."

"Of course."

We started along the edge of the creek, following the water as it curved through the trees. A narrow dirt trail branched off ahead, worn but unused, disappearing into the weeds around it.

I stopped.

"That path," I said. "Where does it go?"

Talia glanced at it. "Nowhere now. Those trails were here before the subdivision went in. Before that, people used to hike through this area. Now no one does."

I stayed where I was, watching the water slide past, its pace much quicker now.

"Do you mind if I show you something?" Talia asked. "It's a bit of a walk, but I've always thought it was kind of special."

"Lead the way," I said.

She stepped closer to the creek, moving along its bank, and I followed, the dream I'd had pressing against my thoughts.

Follow the water.

Not the path.

To the place where two become one.

We walked in silence until she stopped near a cluster of trees set back from the bank.

"There," she said, pointing.

At first, I didn't see it.

Then I did.

Two trees had grown together at the trunk, their bases fused, branches splitting and rising as one. From the right angle, the shape was unmistakable.

A heart.

"I've always loved that tree," Talia said.

I stepped closer, my gaze dropping to the base of the tree.

The ground behind it had been disturbed at one time. The soil looked like it had shifted, and it was uneven. Even so, someone had been careful, going to a great deal of effort to leave as little of a mark as possible.

I felt a knot of fear in my gut.

"How did you find this place?" I asked.

"My dad brought me here. He used to take me on walks along the creek when I was a kid. This was always our favorite spot."

The words landed with quiet force.

Not a confession.

Not an accusation.

Just a truth, offered without knowing the weight behind it.

I stared at the tree, at the place where two had become one, at the water sliding past.

The dream I had now made sense.

Anne hadn't been hidden far away.

She'd been placed somewhere familiar.

Somewhere only one person thought to look.

I rested my hand against the bark, cold and solid beneath my palm.

Talia looked at me, searching my face.

To her, it was still just a tree that stood out among others in the area.

To me, I had just uncovered answers, and a truth capable of shaking our quiet town to its core.

37

Before we left the creek, I took out my cell phone and walked a slow circle around the tree, careful with my footing, my eyes focused on the ground around me. I took a wide shot first, then another from farther back to capture the curve of the creek and the way the land dipped behind the trunk. I crouched and photographed the base where the soil sat uneven, the place where grass refused to grow the same way it did everywhere else. I took one last photo from the water's edge, with the tree centered in the frame.

Talia eyed me with curiosity, unsure of what I was doing and why, and I didn't have the heart to tell her yet.

"You took a lot of pictures," she said.

"I suppose I did," I said.

I slipped my phone back into my pocket, and she nodded toward the path that led back to her house. We walked in silence for a time, the sound of the creek fading behind us, replaced by the sound of light traffic in the distance.

Halfway back, while Talia walked a few steps ahead, I pulled out my phone again, sending a quick message to Foley and Whitlock.

· · ·

Can you meet me at the Kinkaid house?

I need you here.

I believe I've found evidence pointing to who's responsible for Audrey and Anne's murders.

As we reached the edge of the yard, voices carried through the open kitchen window. Raised. Sharp. Not loud enough to make out the words, but tense enough to stop us both short.

Through the window, I could see Gabriel pacing in the kitchen, his hands slicing through the air as he spoke. Brianne stood near the counter, her shoulders drawn tight, one hand braced against the edge as if she needed something solid to stay upright.

Talia frowned. "What's going on?"

"I'm not sure," I said. "But I'm guessing it may have to do with a conversation I had with your mother earlier."

She took a step closer to the house, peering through the glass. "I've never seen my mom like that. She looks freaked out."

I was almost positive they were talking about Anne. Or about Audrey. Or about the way the two were connected. Either way, their secrets were about to be revealed.

I thought of Talia and the devastation she was about to face, a devastation she didn't even know was coming.

I glanced over at her and said, "Would you do me a favor and wait out here for a few minutes while I talk to your parents?"

Talia raised a brow, surprised. "Is something wrong? If it is, I want to be in there too."

"I just need a few minutes with them."

"Why?"

I met her gaze. "I think they know what happened to Anne."

She tapped a shoe to the ground, thinking. "The more you say her name, the more familiar it is to me. It's like I've heard someone say it before, not too long ago. I just don't remember who said it. Why would my parents know anything about Anne?"

"Because they were at a bonfire with her the night she disappeared. Just give me five minutes, please. I have a better chance of getting them to talk to me if you're not in the room."

It was true, but my thoughts were also on her and what was best for her in that moment.

Her mouth opened, then closed, and I saw fear in her eyes.

"You think they've been hiding something." She looked back at the house, then at me. "It doesn't feel right. I don't like this at all."

"I know, and I'm sorry."

A long moment passed, then she nodded. "Fine. But after five minutes, I'm coming in."

She walked over to a tree in the front yard and leaned against it.

If my suspicions about one or both of her parents were right, her world was about to explode. I was holding the grenade, which felt awful, and I wished there was another way, but there wasn't.

"I'll be right back," I said.

She didn't respond, instead keeping her eyes glued on her parents in the window.

I knocked on the door. They either didn't hear me or didn't care to come to the door, so I let myself inside. As soon as I stepped into the kitchen, the arguing stopped.

Brianne's fists were clenched at her side, her forehead sweaty.

Gabriel stood beside her, looking frustrated.

"We need to talk," I said.

"No, we do not," Brianne said. "Please leave."

"I can't. Not without talking first." I gestured toward the table. "Please, sit down so we can talk."

Brianne glared at Gabriel. "Do something! Make her leave."

"It's time, Brianne," he said. "Time for this to all be over."

Outside, a nervous Talia waited.

Inside, the truth pressed against the walls, ready to break through the moment one of them found the courage to speak.

38

Brianne sat at the table with her hands locked together. Her breathing was fast and jagged, like she was at the start of a panic attack. She tried to speak twice, but nothing came out either time.

Gabriel sat next to her, his shoulders slumped, gaze fixed on the floor. He looked tired, but he also looked relieved, like a weight had been dragging behind him for a long time, and I'd come along and cut the chain.

I remained standing at first, watching the two of them, waiting to hear what they would say. When it became clear neither of them knew where to start, I said, "What happened to Anne?"

Brianne pressed her lips together, then shook her head.

Gabriel raised his gaze to mine. "It was me."

Brianne jerked in her chair. "Gabriel, don't."

He ignored the comment and continued. "The night of the bonfire, Anne left with me."

Brianne buried her head in her hands.

I glanced outside to check on Talia, who was still leaned

against the tree, her expression telling me she was growing impatient.

Turning back to Gabriel, I said, "Will you start from the beginning?"

Gabriel swallowed, then nodded. "As you know, Anne was at the bonfire with us and several others in our friend group. We were all drinking and having a good time. Well, at first."

"Gabriel, stop talking," Brianne said. "You don't have to say anything."

"I do, though," he replied. "I should have done it from the start."

"I heard Anne was talking to you at the bonfire," I said.

"Yes, and I'll admit, there was some flirting between the two of us. After things got heated and everyone started arguing, I just wanted to get out of there, but Anne didn't want to go home yet. She told me she was staying with her aunt, but her aunt was working a graveyard shift that night and wouldn't be home for a while."

"What did you say?"

"Given how late it was, I didn't know where to take her, so I asked if she wanted to see an old, abandoned cabin. I had seen it once before, and I thought ... well, I don't know what I thought."

Brianne rose halfway out of her chair. "Gabriel, enough. You will not say another word until I speak to you in private."

He glanced over at her. "We've had twenty-five years. Anne hasn't."

Brianne slammed her fist against the table. "You are going to destroy everything!"

"It's already been destroyed."

She sank back into her chair, shaking, and I tried to get the conversation back on track. "You were saying you took Anne to the cabin."

He nodded.

"It was a nice night, and I thought a walk through the woods was a good idea, so I parked, grabbed my flashlight and a couple of beers, and we started walking."

"Were the two of you drunk?"

"We'd had a few drinks, so yeah, I'd say we were both tipsy enough to be careless."

"*Careless*," Brianne repeated, as if the word disgusted her.

"Anyway, we were walking toward the cabin, and I just, I had this urge to kiss her. I took her in my arms, leaned her against a tree, and I did. And just so you know, I asked for her permission before I did it. The kiss was mutual."

Brianne's eyes were wide with fury, but she said nothing.

"How long did you stay there?" I asked.

"Not long, a few minutes."

"And then you kept walking?"

He nodded. "We made it to the cabin and went in. I was telling jokes, and she was laughing and carving her initials into the wood. We walked back outside and were checking out the area around the cabin. She was about a foot in front of me, and she turned around and reached out like she wanted to take my hand. And ... and she stumbled. She tripped on something. A tree root or a rock. I don't know. It all happened so fast. Next thing I knew, she'd fallen face first to the ground."

As the story unfolded, I could see it in my mind, clear and concise. He could have been leaving things out or leading me astray and telling me the version he wanted me to believe, but the story was solid, and I had no reason to believe otherwise.

"What happened after she fell?" I asked.

"There was a boulder half buried in the dirt. She hit it so hard when she went down, I heard it."

He stared at the table, grief-stricken and filled with remorse.

"I shone my flashlight on her," he said. "And there was blood. So much blood."

Brianne glared at him. "Think about our daughter, Gabriel. Think about what you're about to put her through."

"Talia is outside," I said, my voice low. "I asked her to allow me a few minutes to talk to you first. I thought it might be easier."

Brianne spun toward me, wild-eyed, voice raised. "What did you say to her?"

"She knows the two of you were with Anne the night she died, but not much more than that." I faced Gabriel. "Continue."

"As soon as I realized what had happened to Anne, I knelt beside her," he said. "She looked at me and tried to say something, and then she closed her eyes, and she was ... she was gone."

"And you panicked."

Gabriel's composure broke. "I was eighteen. I was stupid. I was terrified. I thought if I told the police, they'd make up their own story and say I raped her and then killed her. I thought of my parents. I thought of my life ending before it even started. I thought of everyone making me out to be some kind of monster."

"And that mattered more to you than the truth. Did you rape her?"

"No, of course not."

"But you had sex."

"We did, and before you accuse me of leaving that part out, I was just trying to get through the story first, and then I was going to circle back to the sex part."

"What did you do when you realized she was dead?"

"I ... I wrapped my shirt around her wound to get the blood to stop, then I scooped her up in my arms and took her back inside the cabin. There was a bed inside. A metal frame. The mattress was rotten. I pulled the mattress up and I slid her under the bed."

My stomach lurched, a combination of sadness and unease. "You hid her."

He flinched. "I didn't think of it as hiding. I thought of it as … I don't know. I thought I would put her there until I figured out what to do next."

"Then what happened?"

"I went home. I washed the blood off my hands and scrubbed my body until my skin burned."

I pictured him back then, young and terrified, choosing silence over truth. And I pictured Anne's family, waiting for a loved one they'd never see again.

"What happened the next day?" I asked.

"I grabbed a shovel, and I went back. There was a hole beneath the bed, toward the top. The floorboards were loose in one spot. I dug it several feet deeper, and I put her in it. Then I covered it up, put some of the boards back, and I left."

"The cabin has been torn down," I said. "Found a few bone fragments, but nothing more. If you're telling me the truth, it means at some point, you moved her."

He nodded. "Years passed. I got older. I tried to forget, tried to focus on work, my marriage, our daughter, but the regret stayed with me, locked in my head, a constant reminder of what I'd done."

Brianne's lips trembled, but she stayed quiet.

"Several years ago, I came across a unique tree not far from our property."

"The one shaped like a heart," I said, "where two trees have fused to become one."

He raised a brow. "You know?"

"I do."

"I discovered it while I was walking along the creek. I saw it from the right angle, and it felt like a sign, like it had been put there to mock me. The more I thought about it, the more I realized Anne deserved better than having her remains beneath an old cabin. She deserved a place that wasn't ..."

Gabriel pushed his chair back and stood, his body shaking.

"I know what I did," he said. "And I'm sorry it's taken me this long to confess it. But I'm telling you the truth when I say I had nothing to do with Audrey's murder. I loved that girl. I would never do anything to—"

I raised a hand, stopping him.

"After hearing your story, I know you wouldn't. But you," I said, turning toward Brianne. "I believe you would."

A sharp, painful scream ripped through the room, and I looked back, seeing Talia standing several feet behind us, eyes wide as she said, "*Mom?*"

39

The room felt like all the air had been sucked out of it.

Brianne was the first to speak, her tone stern. "I didn't kill Audrey. How could you even accuse me of such a thing?"

Talia began sobbing, folding in on herself as if her body could no longer support her weight.

Gabriel reached for her.

"Don't!" Talia cried. "Don't touch me."

The words hit him hard, as his hands fell back to his sides, his expression grim. "Please, Talia, I would never—"

She shook her head. "I feel like I don't even know you, either of you."

Up to now, I wasn't sure how much of our previous conversation Talia had overheard. Now I knew it was enough.

Brianne stood, her movements stiff and controlled.

"This is insane," she said, turning toward me. "You've got some nerve coming into my house, accusing me of murdering a girl I loved."

"She's right," Gabriel said. "Audrey was like a daughter to us. Brianne would never hurt her."

I held my ground, looking Brianne in the eye. "Earlier, when I first arrived and we were talking, your behavior was far different than the visit we had before. I sensed something—fear—and your need to control the narrative, to spin things in a way that had me looking anywhere else, as long as it's away from you and your family. That alone tells me you're hiding something."

"That's not—"

"You asked me why Anne matters so much in my investigation," I said. "But I believe you know why. If Audrey figured out who Anne was and what happened to her, there was a good chance she'd also figure out who killed her. I believe Gabriel's story about Anne's death being an accident. I also believe he'd rather confess what he did than harm Audrey. *You,* on the other hand ..."

Gabriel tipped his head to the side, narrowing his eyes as he stared at Brianne like he was seeing something he hadn't before.

She turned toward him. "What, Gabriel? Why are you looking at me that way?"

"The detective has it all wrong. Doesn't she?"

Brianne shook her head but said nothing.

"Look me in the eye and tell me she's wrong," he said again, louder this time.

"I ... I ..."

Talia lifted her head, the tears continuing to fall as she looked at her mother. "I remember now."

"What do you remember?" I asked.

"Something I hadn't before. You said her name, Mom. You said Anne's name."

In unison, we turned toward her.

"When?" I asked.

"The day before Audrey died. She came over after school. I was coming down the stairs, and you were talking to Audrey in the kitchen. You didn't see me, not at first."

"What all did you hear?" I asked.

"Audrey said Anne's name and then something about a bonfire. At the time, I didn't think anything of it."

"Is it true, Brianne?" Gabriel asked. "Did Audrey talk to you about Anne?"

Brianne bit down on her bottom lip as tears pooled in her eyes, tears she seemed determined not to let fall. She looked at Talia, then at Gabriel, and then at me, her expression now resigned. "Audrey came to me, and she started asking questions about everyone in our friend group from high school. She mentioned the cabin, finding a locket, and something else, though she didn't say what. I was just ... I was trying to protect you, to protect our family."

Talia leaned against the wall, her head shaking. "You killed her! You killed my best friend to protect your secret, and Dad's. How could you?"

"Oh, honey, I'm so sorry," Brianne said. "I know there's nothing I can say to ease your pain. I was scared, and I ... I didn't know what else to do. She was sure Anne had been murdered, and she planned on going to the police with the new evidence she'd found. I tried talking her out of it, but it didn't work. There was nothing I could say to change her mind."

As Brianne's confession settled in, Gabriel buried his head in his hands.

"I can't believe that this is ... what *you*, what you did to her," Talia said.

"I'm sorry," Brianne said. "I never meant for either of you to find out about—"

"Stop! Just stop it! I don't want to hear anymore! I'm going to be sick!"

Talia slapped her hand against her mouth and screamed. Then she turned and ran upstairs, slamming a door behind her.

Brianne turned toward me. "I just did what I thought I had to do. Now I wish I could go back and fix everything."

But she couldn't go back.

A sweet girl had been denied the chance to live out her life, all because of a horrible secret.

Outside, the sound of tires crunching over gravel cut through the room.

Headlights flashed through the front windows.

Foley and Whitlock had arrived.

40

Whitlock stepped in first and took in the scene, his eyes landing on Gabriel standing near the table, Brianne seated, pale and hollow-eyed. Foley entered behind him, his eyes narrowed as he clocked all the faces.

"Somber crowd," Whitlock said.

Foley turned toward me. "Care to explain what's going on here?"

I nodded and began, starting from the moment Gabriel admitted Anne left the bonfire with him, to the cabin, to the fall, to the years of silence, to the truth now sitting between us like a live wire. Then I continued with Brianne and her confession.

When I finished, both Foley and Whitlock had moved their hands to their hips, heads shaking.

"I say, it's a lot to take in, isn't it?" Whitlock said.

I turned to Gabriel. "There's something you haven't admitted yet."

He looked at me, offering a slight nod.

I continued.

"Your wife has always known about what happened to Anne. And yet, you left her out of the story."

Gabriel didn't answer right away. He turned toward his wife, searching her face, his expression desperate and broken.

Brianne met his gaze.

"It's okay," she said. "You don't have to protect me anymore. Yes, I knew. I've always known. He called me that night, right after Anne fell. I was his best friend long before I was his wife, you see."

"What did he say?" I asked.

"He was terrified. He told me what happened, and he said he didn't know what to do."

"You told me to calm down," Gabriel said. "You told me—"

"I told you I'd find a way to get to you, and I snuck out of the house and met you at the cabin."

Foley straightened.

Whitlock's jaw tightened.

"It was all my idea," Brianne continued.

"Brianne, don't," Gabriel said.

"It's all over now," she said. "It doesn't matter."

I crossed my arms and leaned against the counter. "What was your idea?"

"I told him not to go to the police."

"Why not?"

"He was drunk. I didn't think they'd believe it was an accident. I thought if he confessed, they might not believe him, and it would ruin his life."

"You said—" his voice cracked. "You said burying her was my only option."

"I said it would protect you," she replied. "And it did, until now."

I turned toward Gabriel. "You may not have murdered Anne, but you had a chance to do the right thing, and you didn't. You did what Brianne suggested, and you buried Anne in that dilapidated cabin. And you lived with that."

"I know, and I'm sorry."

I shifted my gaze to Brianne. "And *you*. Audrey came to you because she trusted you, and I'm guessing she suspected someone in the friend group killed Anne, but she never expected it to be you. And you rewarded that trust by taking her life."

Brianne swallowed. "She knew enough to be dangerous. Once she went to the police, once they reopened the investigation, I was sure they'd find a way to trace her back to Gabriel, forensics being what they are nowadays."

"You should have told me," Gabriel said. "I would never have allowed you to go through with your plan."

"That's the reason I didn't."

"All this time, you've been mourning Audrey, acting as though her death struck you as hard as it did her own mother," I said. "It's disgusting."

Hands trembling, Gabriel faced his wife. "You destroyed us. You destroyed our family."

"Don't blame me," Brianne said. "If you hadn't taken Anne into the woods that night, none of this would be happening."

Foley stepped forward. "I believe we've heard enough. Gabriel and Brianne, you're coming with us."

They didn't flinch or resist or hesitate.

Whitlock read them their rights and took them into custody, and as the door closed behind them, my thoughts turned to Talia and the truths that had been exposed at long last.

41

I ascended the stairs, each step seeming heavier and more difficult than the one before it. Talia's door was shut when I reached it.

I knocked, saying, "It's Georgiana."

"Are you alone?"

"Yes."

"Okay, come in."

When I opened the door, the room was dim, the curtains pulled halfway closed. A record played low in the background, the needle crackling between notes.

Coldplay.

The sound filled the space without demanding attention.

Talia lay stretched across her bed, staring at the ceiling, one arm draped over her eyes.

"I love this album," I said.

"It was Audrey's favorite. She used to say it made everything feel less heavy."

I crossed the room and sat on the edge of the bed.

"I was wondering how you were doing, but it's a bit of an

obvious question, so I won't. I'll just say, I'm sorry. I wish I would have been wrong about everything."

She moved her arm from her eyes, flopping it over the side of the bed.

"I saw the police pull up outside," she said, her voice raw. "Is it over? Have my parents been arrested?"

"Yes, they have," I said. "It's over. I'm not sure what the charges will be for your father, but I'm sorry to say they'll be charging your mother with murder. I'm so sorry, Talia."

She offered a slow nod, as if my words needed time to land.

"I keep thinking I should feel something," she said. "Anger. Relief. Hate. But I'm just numb. I feel dead inside."

"It's normal," I said. "I've been through it before."

She turned her head, looking at me. "How was my dad when they arrested him? Did he say anything?"

"He asked me to tell you that he loves you, and that he's sorry."

"Yeah, well, sorry doesn't change what happened, does it?"

"Your mom—"

"If she said anything, I don't want to hear it."

"I understand."

The record shifted from one song to the next.

"Is there anything I can do for you?" I asked. "Or any questions you have now that you know the truth?"

She gave the question some thought.

"Do you think my dad was telling the truth, about what happened with Anne?" she asked. "I mean, he's always been the gentlest soul. I don't know how to feel about what he did or how to process it."

"It will take time, and that's okay. As for your father's story, I believe he was telling the truth. He just left out the part about your mother being involved because he was trying to protect her. He didn't know she killed Audrey. As for his gentle soul, I feel it. The way he handled Anne wasn't right, but I choose to believe he's been wanting to make it right for a long time."

Talia let out a long, jagged breath. "I don't know what I'm supposed to do now. This house feels different, almost like I don't belong here anymore, trapped in a home full of secrets and lies."

"I don't think you should be alone tonight."

She hesitated. "Maybe not, but I'm not good company for anyone."

"I disagree," I said. "I think you're the perfect company for a certain someone."

She raised a brow. "Who?"

"Logan," I said. "He's at my house. He lost his girlfriend, the love of his life, and you lost your best friend. The two of you don't need to carry the pain of it alone, not when you have each other."

"I wouldn't even know where to begin or what to say to him."

"I wouldn't worry about all that right now," I said. "Just sitting in the same room together is sometimes enough."

As the record came to a stop, she pushed herself into a sitting position.

"Okay," she said. "But just for tonight."

"That's all I'm asking."

She ran a hand along her face and stood, slipping on a jacket, and turning the record player off.

As the room fell quiet, she followed me downstairs, pausing on the porch and turning to look at the house behind her.

"I don't think I can come back here for a while," she said.

"That's fine," I said. "I'll be here to help you, whatever you need, all right?"

She nodded, then followed me to the car.

We pulled away, and the house faded into the dark behind us.

And she didn't look back.

Not once.

42

One month later, the town was still reeling.

Not in a loud way, and not with spectacle. Cambria absorbed shock the way it always had, through hushed conversations in grocery aisles, lowered voices at coffee counters, and the careful way people chose their words when names came up that no longer felt safe to say aloud.

Two people everyone thought they knew.

Two crimes separated by decades.

And a single truth that had been waiting for the right moment to surface.

At long last, Anne Fontaine's name was spoken without speculation attached to it. Audrey's death was no longer a mystery shaped by rumor. Justice, such as it was, had come late and imperfect, but it had come.

After the truth came out, Talia worried at first that the town would turn on her, that her parents' actions would stain her by association. But I knew otherwise.

People showed up.

They checked in.

They left notes on her car.

Brought her flowers and food.

They made it clear, in quiet ways, that love could survive even the worst kind of truth. Talia wasn't part of her parents' crimes, and she wouldn't be punished for their actions.

Talia moved into Audrey's parents' house within days of everything coming out. It made sense to her, she said. The rooms still held Audrey's presence, and the grief she felt was easier when shared with others as they tried to move forward together, one unsteady step at a time.

When I'd last checked in on her a couple of days ago, she looked stronger than I expected.

Not healed.

Not whole.

But working on getting through each day.

She told me she spent most of her free time with Logan now, who was back at home with his parents. For her birthday, he'd sketched a portrait of Audrey, one he had worked on while staying at my house. Talia said she cried when she opened it, then cried again when she hung it on the wall.

It wasn't closure. It was something else. A reminder that love didn't vanish just because the person was gone.

Gabriel had been charged with involuntary manslaughter, abuse of a corpse, and failure to report a death, among other things.

As my thoughts shifted to the present moment, I turned onto a familiar street and slowed down as Violet Fontaine's house came into view. I parked behind Bear's truck. He had arrived before me and stood beside it now, his hands tucked into his jacket pockets, shoulders tight.

In the last month, Violet had learned the truth. Not just about Anne, but about Bear and the possibility that he was her half-brother. A DNA test confirmed it, and she'd asked if the two of them could meet. Bear had kept putting it off, saying he was nervous, so I'd stepped in, offering to make formal introductions.

I got out of the car and walked over to him.

"You know something," I said. "You've never told me your actual name."

He shot me a wink. "I prefer Bear. It's a good nickname."

"Understood. You ready?"

He exhaled, then nodded. "As ready as I'm going to get."

We walked to the door together, and Bear slowed near the porch, hesitating for half a second. I reached for the doorbell, pressing it before he had the chance to change his mind.

The door opened, and Violet's eyes landed on me first. Then she saw Bear, and she stepped forward without hesitation and wrapped her arms around me.

"Thank you," she said, her voice thick, "for helping make today happen."

I nodded and turned. "This is Bear."

Violet studied his face with care, as he swallowed, his jaw tight, eyes fixed on hers.

"I—" he started, then stopped.

She reached out, grabbing his hand.

"Come in," she said. "Please."

They entered the house together, still hand in hand. Bear glanced back at me once, his expression one of relief.

I said goodbye, and as the door closed behind them, I remained on the porch for a time, thinking about all that had happened since the case began.

Anne had been brought home at last.

Audrey's voice had been heard, even in death.

And two lives that had grown in parallel without knowing it had crossed in ways no one could imagine.

Some stories ended with justice.

Others ended with mercy.

This one ended with both.

And as I turned away from the house and walked back to my car, I thought about truth and how it always finds a way to come out in the end. And when it does, it changes everything.

THE END

Thank you for reading Little Silent Stranger, book 13 in the Georgiana Germaine Mystery Series. I hope you enjoyed getting to know the characters in this story as much as I enjoyed writing them for you. You can find the series order (as of the date of this printing) in the "Books by Cheryl Bradshaw" section below.

...

In LITTLE BITTER TRUTHS (Georgiana Germaine, Book 14)

The wrong sister is murdered, leaving the right one in grave danger ...

When Willow Bennett asks her identical twin, Wren, to house-sit while she's away on a work trip, a small favor turns deadly when Wren is found murdered in Willow's bed.

. . .

Grief turns to terror when the truth becomes impossible to ignore, and Willow realizes she was the killer's target, not Wren.

Desperate for justice, Willow turns to Private Investigator Georgiana Germaine. What begins as a case of mistaken identity soon turns to a web of secrets, old wounds, and a motive no one saw coming.

As Georgiana digs deeper, time is not on her side. The killer already struck once, a fatal mistake that's about to be corrected.

...

You Can Read a Sneak Peek of Chapter One and Reserve Your Copy of Little Bitter Truths in Cheryl's Store at CherylBradshawStore.Com

ENJOY LITTLE
SILENT STRANGER?

You can show your appreciation by leaving a review on Amazon, Barnes & Noble, Apple Books, Google Play, Kobo, or Goodreads.

If you write a review, please be sure to email Cheryl (cheryl@authorcherylbradshaw(dot)com) so she can express her gratitude. She does her best to reply to as many emails as she can, and she appreciates every piece of mail she receives.

ABOUT CHERYL BRADSHAW

Cheryl Bradshaw is a New York Times and 16-time USA Today bestselling author writing in multiple genres, including mystery, thriller, romantic suspense, supernatural suspense, and poetry. She is a Shamus Award finalist for best private eye novel of the year, an eFestival of Words winner for best thriller, and has published over fifty books since 2011.

When she's not writing, Cheryl loves jet-setting to new countries, playing with her grandkids, high tea, and pursuing a wishful side career as a professional food tester of wine and cheese.

NEVER MISS ONE OF CHERYL'S BOOK'S AGAIN!

Sign up for Cheryl Bradshaw's "Killer Newsletter" today to be the first to know when a new book is released and to enter to win fun bookish swag. You'll also receive some fantastic book freebies just for joining!

Learn more by visiting CherylBradshawStore.Com and adding your email address on the SIGN UP AND SAVE form at the bottom of the home page. Your email in for our eyes only and will not be shared with anyone else.

BOOKS BY CHERYL BRADSHAW

Sloane Monroe Series

Silent as the Grave (Prequel, Book 0)

When the body of Rebecca Barlow is found floating in the lake, private investigator Sloane Monroe takes on her very first homicide.

Black Diamond Death (Book 1)

Charlotte Halliwell has a secret. But before revealing it to her sister, she's found dead.

Murder in Mind (Book 2)

A woman is found murdered, the serial killer's trademark "S" carved into her wrist.

I Have a Secret (Book 3)

Doug Ward has been running from his past for twenty years. But after his fourth whisky of the night, he doesn't want to keep quiet, not anymore.

Stranger in Town (Book 4)

A frantic mother runs down the aisles, searching for her missing daughter. But little Olivia is already gone.

Bed of Bones (Book 5) (USA Today Bestselling Book)

Sometimes even the deepest, darkest secrets find their way to the surface.

Flirting with Danger (Book 5.5) A Sloane Monroe Short Story

A fancy hotel. A weekend getaway. For Sloane Monroe, rest has finally arrived, until the lights go out, a woman screams, and Sloane's nightmare begins.

Hush Now Baby (Book 6) (USA Today Bestselling Book)

Serena Westwood tiptoes to her baby's crib and looks inside, startled to find her newborn son is gone.

Dead of Night (Book 6.5) A Sloane Monroe Short Story

After her mother-in-law is fatally stabbed, Wren is seen fleeing with the bloody knife. Is Wren the killer, or is a dark, scandalous family secret to blame?

Gone Daddy Gone (Book 7) (USA Today Bestselling Book)

A man lurks behind Shelby in the park. Who is he? And why does he have a gun?

Smoke & Mirrors (Book 8) (USA Today Bestselling Book)

Grace Ashby wakes to the sound of a horrifying scream. She races down the hallway, finding her mother's lifeless body on the floor in a pool of blood. Her mother's boyfriend Hugh is hunched over her, but is Hugh really her mother's killer?

...

Sloane Monroe Stories: Deadly Sins

...

Deadly Sins: Sloth (Book 1)

Darryl has been shot, and a mysterious woman is sprawled out on the floor in his hallway. She's dead too. Who is she? And why have they both been murdered?

Deadly Sins: Wrath (Book 2)

Headlights flash through Maddie's car's back windshield, someone following close behind. When her car careens into a nearby tree, the chase comes to an end. But for Maddie, the end is just the beginning.

Deadly Sins: Lust (Book 3)

Marissa Calhoun sits alone on a beach-like swimming hole nestled on Australia's foreshore. Tonight, the lagoon is hers and hers alone. Or is it?

Deadly Sins: Greed (Book 4)

It was just another day for mob boss Giovanni Luciana until he took his car for a drive.

Deadly Sins: Envy (Book 5)

A cryptic message. A missing niece. And only twenty-four hours to pay.

Deadly Sins: Pride (Book 6)

A secret lies within the Kingston mansion's walls, a secret that's about to bring the past into the present.

Deadly Sins: Gluttony (Book 7)

In a town where silence holds its own dark voice, the past has returned, and Gideon Belmont is about to learn an unfortunate lesson.

...

Sloane & Maddie, Peril Awaits (Co-Authored with Janet Fix)

...

The Silent Boy (Book 1)

In the hallway of a local tavern, six-year old Louie Alvarez waits for his mother to take him home. A scream rips through the air, followed by the sound of a gun being fired. Louie freezes, then turns, with a single thought on his mind: RUN.

The Shadow Children (Book 2)

Within the tunnels of the historic port city of Savannah, fourteen-year-old

Andi Leland has her mind set on freedom—not just for herself but for all the other teens who have come before her.

The Broken Soul (Book 3)

When the party of a lifetime becomes a party to the death, the lines become blurred. Friends become enemies. Drugs become weapons. And that's just the beginning.

The Widow Maker (Book 4)

A friend murdered. A business in trouble. A marriage struggling to survive. And that's just the beginning.

The Familiar Stranger (Book 5)

As semi-retired private detective Sloane Monroe unwinds at a luxurious spa retreat in North Carolina, a jarring phone call shatters her peaceful getaway.

...

Georgiana Germaine Series

...

Little Girl Lost (Book 1)

For the past two years, former detective Georgiana "Gigi" Germaine has been living off the grid, until today, when she hears some disturbing news that shakes her.

Little Lost Secrets (Book 2)

When bones are discovered inside the walls during a home renovation, Georgiana uncovers a secret that's linked to her father's untimely death thirty years earlier.

Little Broken Things (Book 3)

Twenty-year-old Olivia Spencer sits at her desk in her mother's bookshop, dreaming about her upcoming wedding. The store may be closed, but she's not alone, and her dream is about to become her worst nightmare.

Little White Lies (Book 4)

When a serial killer sweeps through the streets of Cambria, California, Georgiana Germaine gets swept up into a tangled web of deception and lies.

Little Tangled Webs (Book 5)

What if you knew the person you loved was murdered, but no one else believed you? Eighteen-year-old Harper Ellis knows she's right, and she's prepared to risk her life to prove it.

Little Shattered Dreams (Book 6)

At fifty-five, Quinn Abernathy has been through her fair share of experiences in life. And tonight, her past is coming back to haunt her.

Little Last Words (Book 7)

After living in a verbally abusive relationship for the past six years, twenty-seven-year-old Penelope Barlow has finally found the courage to leave. But can she escape ... with her life?

Little Buried Secrets (Book 8)

In a split-second, a car collides with Margot, and she finds herself hurdling through the air, her bike going one way as she goes the other. Her mind whirls in this moment, as she thinks about her life and just how much she doesn't want to die.

Little Stolen Memories (Book 9)

In a secluded cabin deep within the woods, an ominous stranger is about to change the lives of six unsuspecting teenagers forever.

Little Empty Promises (Book 10)

As librarian Cordelia Bennett prepares to lock up for the night, a mysterious sound startles her. She turns. The fading light reveals a chilling presence in the shadows, and Cordelia realizes she's not alone.

Little Hidden Fears (Book 11)

Noelle Winters has just thrown the perfect engagement party ... or so she believes. As the evening winds down and the toast is about the commence, the lights go out. And for someone, the night has just turned deadly.

Little Dark Deeds (Book 12)

It's Georgiana Germaine's wedding day. But when one of her closest friends is noticeably absent from the ceremony, Georgiana worries something sinister is to blame.

Little Silent Stranger (Book 13)

Walking the wooded path to her friend's house, Audrey Ashford soon realizes she's not alone. What begins as a familiar shortcut quickly turns into a deadly encounter, and by the time she reaches the ridge, it's far too late.

Little Bitter Truths (Book 14)

When Willow Bennett asks her identical twin, Wren, to house-sit while she's away on a work trip, a small favor turns deadly when Wren is found murdered in Willow's bed.

...

Margaret Montague Series

Eye for Revenge (USA Today Bestselling Book) (Book 1)

Quinn Montgomery wakes to find herself in the hospital. Her childhood best friend Evie is dead, and Evie's four-year-old son witnessed it all. Traumatized over what he saw, he hasn't spoken.

The Killing Hour (USA Today Bestselling Book) (Book 2)

Suburban housewife Juliette Granger has been living a secret life ... a life that's about to turn deadly for everyone she loves.

<u>The Perfect Lie </u>(Book 3)

When true-crime writer Alexandria Weston is found murdered on the last stop of her book tour, fellow writer Joss Jax steps in to investigate.

<u>Hickory Dickory Dead </u>(USA Today Bestselling Book) (Book 4)

Maisie Fezziwig wakes to a harrowing scream outside. Curious, she walks outside to investigate, and Maisie stumbles on a grisly murder that will change her life forever.

...

Addison Lockhart Series

...

Grayson Manor Haunting (Book 1)

When Addison Lockhart inherits Grayson Manor after her mother's untimely death, she unlocks a secret that's been kept hidden for over fifty years.

Rosecliff Manor Haunting (Book 2)

Addison Lockhart jolts awake. The dream had seemed so real. Eleven-year-old twins Vivian and Grace were so full of life, but they couldn't be They've been dead for over forty years.

Blackthorn Manor Haunting (Book 3)

Addison Lockhart leans over the manor's window, gasping when she feels a hand on her back. She grabs the windowsill to brace herself, but it's too late-- she's already falling.

Belle Manor Haunting (Book 4)

A vehicle barrels through the stop sign, slamming into the car Addison

Lockhart is inside before fleeing the scene. Who is the driver of the other car? And what secrets within the walls of Belle Manor will provide the answer?

Crawley Manor Haunting (Book 5)

Something evil is coming. Something dark. Something seeking to destroy everything and everyone in its path. And Addison Lockhart is the only one who can stop it.

...

Till Death do us Part Novella Series

...

Whispers of Murder (Book 1)

It was Isabelle Donnelly's wedding day, a moment in time that should have been the happiest in her life...until it ended in murder.

Echoes of Murder (Book 2)

When two women are found dead at the same wedding, medical examiner Reagan Davenport will stop at nothing to discover the identity of the killer.

...

www.ingramcontent.com/pod-product-compliance
Lightning Source LLC
Chambersburg PA
CBHW060303310726
48976CB00007B/2196